#5

MW00413642

THOU
SHALT
KILL

A murder by crucifixion unsettles a sleepy town

JOHN DEAN

THE
BOOK
FOLKS

Paperback published by The Book Folks

London, 2018

ISBN 978-1-7268-0279-6

www.thebookfolks.com

Thou Shalt Kill is the fifth stand-alone novel in a series of British murder mysteries featuring Detective Chief Inspector Jack Harris. A full list of the other books is available at the end of this one.

Also to be found at the end of this book is a list of characters.

Chapter one

The late summer sun was beginning to sink slowly behind the hills that cradled Levton Bridge when the four young people arrived at the church. After taking a few seconds to compose their thoughts, they pushed their way through the heavy oak door and walked into the 18th century building, the air thick with dampness despite the warmth of the September evening.

The chill of the air was matched by the chill of their reception, and the young people stood uncertainly at the entrance for a few moments, surveying the group of people lined up at the far end of the church, each one of them eying the new arrivals in solemn silence. Most of the group was retired, and their stern faces were partly obscured by the shadows cast by the row of flickering candles that had been lined up next to the altar.

'Here goes nothing,' said David Fulton, a smartly-dressed man in his mid-twenties, with short-cropped hair.

'They have to learn, David,' said a young man with long hair. 'We have to find a way to return them to the one true path.'

'Amen to that,' said Fulton.

1

He looked at the others and started to walk slowly down the aisle, his footsteps echoing on the cold stone floor. When he was halfway down the aisle, a white-haired man in grey slacks and a green woollen jumper stepped forward and held up a hand to bar Fulton's way to the altar.

'That's quite far enough,' said Dennis McGuffin. 'We told you last time that you are not welcome here.'

'This is the House of the Lord,' said Fulton. He continued to approach McGuffin until the men were standing six feet apart, where he stopped. 'All are welcome here, and all are loved.'

The other young people, two women and the long-haired man, who was in his late teens, nodded their agreement.

'Yes, well, you are still not welcome. You are a disruptive influence.'

'All we want to do is praise the Lord.'

'Yes, well do it somewhere else,' said Edie Prentice, an elderly woman in a pale blue cardigan and a tweed jacket. She jabbed a finger at him. 'We don't want you. We don't want any of you.'

'Maybe it *would* be best if you do it somewhere else,' said Henry Grace, who was in his late sixties with wispy grey hair and thick-rimmed spectacles. He tried to strike a more conciliatory note; Henry Grace was not a man who sought confrontation. 'We do not want to fall out with you.'

'Don't waste your breath, Henry,' said McGuffin. 'You can't reason with these people.'

'What do you think, Jim?' asked David Fulton. He looked at the vicar, who was standing in the midst of the congregation and appeared to be uncomfortable at the exchange. 'Did your training suggest that turning away true believers from the House of God is the right thing to do?'

The vicar, a slim, red-haired and bearded man in his early thirties, looked unhappily at him. He seemed to be struggling to form words.

'I think there are ways of couching your views so that they do not cause so much offence,' he said. 'Henry's right, we don't want to fall out, but this really is not the place for you.'

'And you truly believe that, do you?'

The vicar looked at the stern expressions on the faces of his congregation.

'I am afraid I do, David,' he said eventually in a voice that was hardly audible.

The young people murmured their disapproval, a smattering of applause rippled through the congregation, and the vicar stared at the floor, his head bowed so that they could not see the tears that were starting in his eyes.

'Don't waste your breath on them,' said McGuffin. 'They're not living in the real world. All this talk of building a new hall to cope with the rush of new members is pie in the sky. Who on earth would come here?'

'They will when we tell them that the spirit of the Lord truly dwells in this place,' said Fulton. His voice trembled with emotion. 'This will be a place of pilgrimage. Of spiritual rebirth.'

'You're talking rubbish, lad!' exclaimed McGuffin. 'And even if they do come, where's the money going to come from to accommodate them?'

'The Lord will provide.'

'Balderdash!' exclaimed McGuffin. 'I told you this last time, lad, there's no way Jesus is going to come down from Heaven wielding a bloody chequebook. He didn't when the roof started leaking and he won't now.'

'If you have faith, anything is possible, Dennis.'

'Enough!' said McGuffin. 'As chairman of the Parochial Church Council, I am banning you from this church!'

'You do not have that kind of authority,' said Fulton calmly. He looked at the clergyman. 'Only the Lord can bar people from his presence, and he will always forgive. Isn't that right, Jim?'

The vicar opened his mouth as if to speak but a look from McGuffin silenced him.

'Think who pays your salary, Reverend,' he said.

Fulton shook his head sadly, and he and his friends turned and left the church in silence. When they had gone, McGuffin turned to the vicar.

'I ask you again, Jim,' he said. 'Did they come here because you invited them? We all know that you have sympathies with their crackpot beliefs.'

'I keep telling you, no,' said the vicar. Infused with sudden anger, he looked round at the congregation. 'But that does not mean that what you have done tonight is right. David is correct; all are welcome in the House of the Lord.'

'I knew that appointing you was a mistake,' scowled McGuffin.

And with that, he shot the vicar a contemptuous look and stalked wordlessly from the building, followed by the congregation. One person held back for a few moments, a dark-haired woman in her thirties who made sure that the others had gone before she walked up the vicar and reached out to touch him gently on the arm.

'I'm still with you,' said Anne Gerrard. 'Maybe this is not the end but the beginning.'

She patted his arm and followed the others out into the night. When she had gone, Jim Miles could contain the emotion no more and stood in the shadows of the church with tears streaming down his cheeks, sobs racking his body and echoing around the empty building. Eventually, he sank to his knees and held his hands together in prayer.

'Where are you?' he cried.

But answer came there none.

* * *

Dusk was falling gently over the allotments on the edge of Levton Bridge when the first nail drove hard into the man's right hand and into the door frame of the shed, tearing through bone and sinew and ripping into the timber. The second nail did the same thing on his left hand a few moments later, sending blood spurting high into the air. The victim's agonised screams pierced the stillness of the late summer evening air as he begged for mercy and struggled desperately to free himself as the man with the hammer drew it back to strike a third blow.

For a second, time stood still then the hammer drove forwards; the victim fell silent, and his writhing ceased as his assailant sent the third nail smashing through his forehead, splitting the skull and piercing his brain. The victim twitched for a few moments then was still. His suffering was at an end.

'Vengeance be mine, saith the Lord,' murmured the killer.

'Amen to that brother,' said the man who had held the struggling victim as the nails were driven in. 'Amen to that indeed.'

They stood and surveyed their handiwork with satisfaction for a few moments then crossed themselves and glanced at the sky, their hands held together in prayer, lips moving in silent devotion. As lights started to go on in the nearby houses and back doors opened, the men walked with steady and unhurried steps towards the gate, neither speaking. The only sound was the gentle clucking of the chickens in their coop on a neighbouring plot, followed a couple of minutes later by the wailing of sirens carried on the night air.

It had begun.

Chapter two

'They're hotbeds of feuding, are allotments,' said Detective Sergeant Matt Gallagher. He nodded wisely as he stood and surveyed the crucified body, which was illuminated by the harsh glow of the arc light set up in front of the shed. 'Absolute bloody hotbeds.'

'Maybe they are,' replied Detective Chief Inspector Jack Harris. 'But it's a big step from arguments over the onions to nailing someone to a door, Matty lad.'

'Too late for onions,' said Gallagher.

'What?'

'Too late for onions.'

'And you're an expert, are you?'

'I used to have one of these places when I worked in the Met. Loved it. Bloody loved it. In fact, I've been on the waiting list here for eight months. You have to wait for someone to die before you get one...' The sergeant's voice tailed off when he realised what he'd said. 'Oops. Motive?'

Harris said nothing but allowed himself a smile. In the two years since the sergeant had moved from the Metropolitan Police to work in the North Pennines town, the inspector had learnt to tolerate Gallagher's ways and realised that his flashes of humour could lighten a dark mood. And looking at the dead man, the inspector's mood was as dark as they came.

'Anyway,' said Gallagher after a few moments, 'I am just saying that onions are usually over by this time of year. It's much more likely to be about winter cabbages. Or cauli…'

'Is that all you can think about?' asked the inspector. His tolerance of other people never lasted long. 'This isn't Gardeners' World.'

'I'm just saying.'

'Yes, well, don't. Besides, he's hardly dressed for a spot of digging, is he?' Harris watched the forensics team busying themselves around the dead man, who was wearing a dark suit, a white shirt heavily stained with blood and a tie at half-mast. 'What time was it reported?'

'Half an hour, forty minutes ago.' Gallagher glanced at the lights glowing brightly in the windows of the houses that stood beyond the allotments' wire fence. 'Half a dozen people rang in when they heard the screams. Enough to wake the dead, one of them said.'

'He should be so lucky.'

It was 9pm and darkness had fallen over the hill town. There was a slight chill in the air, the first hint that, after the long lazy nights of what been a hot summer, autumn was coming to the northern hills and with it the reminder of winter with its biting winds and driving rain. If Jack Harris stepped back from the arc light and stared across the house roofs, he could just make out beyond the orange glow of street lamps the looming shapes of his beloved hills, visible if he screwed up his eyes and peered hard. He sighed as he always did when work threatened to disrupt his routine of long walks across the tops, his dogs at his heels.

The inspector returned his attention to the dead man and, for a few moments, the two detectives stood in silence.

'It's a hell of a thing,' said Gallagher, serious now. He shook his head. 'I've never seen anything quite like it.'

'What not even in Da Smoke?' Harris gave him a sly look. 'Surely, the mean streets of Bermondsey were packed with folks nailing people to sheds? Sodom and Gomorrah, I heard.'

'Not even there. Have you ever seen anything like this?'

A memory stirred but Harris did not reply, and the detectives lapsed into silence again. To the casual observer, they were very different men, Jack Harris, strong-jawed, thick brown hair without a hint of grey, Matt Gallagher, a decade younger, smaller, stocky, black hair starting to thin, a man, some said, with the appearance of a monk. Where they connected was in their experience of more death than they would have hoped to see, although even they were disturbed by what they were witnessing now and behind the banter lay a sense of foreboding, an anxiety that they were witnessing the beginning of something terrible.

'It's a very specific way to kill someone, isn't it?' said Gallagher eventually. 'I mean, whoever did it could have smashed his skull in with a shovel. Takes a lot less effort.'

'Indeed.' Harris looked round at the allotment. 'So, what do we think he was doing here when he was attacked?'

'Could be his plot. He could have been doing some watering.' Gallagher looked at the raised beds. 'It's been pretty dry the last few days. Perhaps he came down after work and got jumped. That would explain the suit.'

'Assuming it is his allotment, of course. Do we know who he is?'

'A bloke called Michael Hills.' The sergeant held up a plastic evidence bag, containing a laminated card bearing a photograph showing a thin-faced, balding man in his mid-forties with a prominent nose and sunken eyes. The bottom of the picture showed a tie at half-mast. 'Found this in his jacket pocket. Looks like he's one of your favourite people. It's a National Union of Journalists card.'

'Hills,' murmured Harris. 'Hills. He writes for the Roxham Herald, I think.'

'You met him then?'

'Can't say I have. Just recognise the name.' Harris nodded towards the card. 'That have an address for him then?'

''Fraid not,' said Gallagher. He frowned. 'I'm wondering if it might be a fake, actually. I got the office to run the name through the records, but they could not find anything on him at all. Certainly no one local. They're widening the search.'

'There's got to be something.'

'You'd think so, but he's not on the electoral roll. They checked for Roxham as well and further along the valley – nada. Our Mister Hills does not appear to exist.'

'Well, whoever he is we need to find out what he's doing here.'

'Perhaps he writes the gardening column.'

Harris gave his sergeant a pained look.

'Sorry,' grinned Gallagher, glad of the chance to lift the sombre atmosphere. Not that he would ever admit to Harris, but the sight of the dead man had started his stomach churning. 'But like I say, you'd be amazed at what goes on in allotments.'

'Not sure we've had any reports of serious trouble here, though? A couple of shed break-ins, the odd theft of tools, maybe?'

'Take it from me, it's there,' said Gallagher. 'All bubbling under. When I was working in the Met, we dealt with a murder on an allotment. Two old boys who'd had neighbouring plots for thirty years. They'd never got on, and one of them said the wrong thing one Sunday morning. The other one clobbered him with a garden fork then went back to hoeing his peas while he waited for the police to arrive.'

'An act of passion I can understand, but this, Matty lad?' Harris looked at the body and shook his head. 'This is something else. I take it we don't know if this Hills fellow is a plot holder?'

'Butterfield is trying to track down someone from the committee. The chairman's a bloke called Harry Osborne. She's gone to see him.'

'Much good may it do her. He's a right pernickety bastard is Harry. A real stickler for the rules.'

'He'd make an ideal chairman of an allotments committee then,' said Gallagher. 'They love their rules do allotment committees.'

One of the forensics officers turned away from the shed and held up a long nail for them to examine in the spotlight.

'This is what he used,' she said. 'Found it on the floor. Presumably a spare in case he broke one.'

'It's a big bugger,' said Harris.

'It's some kind of masonry nail.'

'Might help us track down where he bought it.'

'Not so sure. You can get them at a lot of hardware stores. We used a couple to replace a loose tile on the cottage after that storm in April.'

'Any prints?'

'Not that I can find. I reckon that whoever did this was wearing gloves. Quite a few footprints in the dust, though, but whoever did it, went to a lot of trouble to scuff them out. Enough to suggest that two of them dragged him in.'

'Makes sense,' said Gallagher. 'One person could not do this on their own. Any tyre prints?'

'Plenty. Too many. A lot of the plot-holders bring their car along the track, so they're all mixed up. Sorry, guys, but I'm not sure how much help we'll be on this one.'

Harris scowled and walked up to the body. He stared into the tortured face, the tongue lolling to one side, the eyes rolled back.

'What did you do to make someone do this to you then, sunbeam?' he murmured.

The inspector turned round to see a white-haired man in a tweed jacket making his way towards them carrying a leather bag, struggling to keep his footing on the crooked paving stones in the shadows beyond the pool of light cast by the arc lamp.

'Evening, Hawk,' said the Home Office pathologist. He stopped to survey the scene, unable to conceal his astonishment. 'I'll tell you something for free. It wasn't suicide.'

The pathologist winked at Gallagher, and the sergeant laughed.

'The two of you should go on the stage,' sighed Harris, giving them both a world-weary look.

'Sorry,' said the pathologist but the twinkle remained in his eye.

The detectives watched as a young woman with short blonde hair and wearing a dark knee-length coat walked up the path, clutching a piece of paper.

'Is this chummy's plot then?' asked Harris.

'Not according to the chairman,' said Detective Constable Alison Butterfield. She held up the piece of paper. 'Took me ages to get the membership list out of him, mind. He kept asking me if I had a warrant and did I know anything about GDPR?'

'GDPR?' asked Harris blankly.

'The new legislation on data protection? The chief sent a big memo out about it earlier this year.'

Harris still looked nonplussed.

'Anyway,' said Butterfield, 'Harry Osborne tried to make out that under GDPR I could not have his list.'

'Yeah, that sounds like Harry.'

'What's more, he seemed more worried that the veg does not get trampled than he was about the fact that there had been a murder on the allotments. I'm to stress the point.'

'I'll bet you are. There's no one by the name of Michael Hills on his list of tenants then?'

'Nope.' The detective constable handed the piece of paper to the inspector. 'This is plot 34 and, according to the list, it is occupied by a bloke called Dennis McGuffin. He's also on the allotment committee.'

'Yeah, I know Dennis, he's another awkward one, but this is definitely not him.' The inspector held the paper up the light and scanned the rest of the names. 'In fact, I know all of this lot and it's none of them. This is nothing to do with the allotments.'

'You say that,' began Gallagher. 'But when I...'

'If this is another cosy anecdote about your allotment...' said Harris. He did not finish the sentence. He did not need to.

Gallagher shut his mouth, and Butterfield tried not to laugh at the crestfallen expression on the sergeant's face.

'So, what have we got then?' asked Harris. 'Is Michael Hills a journalist who's been killed over something he was investigating or is it something religiously motivated?'

'Not sure that the Roxham Herald has ever investigated anything in its life,' said Gallagher. 'The front page last week was some shite about litter.'

'My money's on the religious motive,' said Butterfield. She gestured at the body. 'Got to be, hasn't it?'

'I suspect you are right,' said Harris gloomily. 'And that makes it a hate crime. The media will love this, especially since he may be one of their own.'

'I'm not so sure about the religious angle,' said Gallagher, unable to contain himself any longer. 'The murder I investigated on the allotments in Bermondsey was caused by a disagreement about leeks.'

'Yeah, folks can get pretty aerated about leeks,' said Butterfield with a nod of the head. 'My dad once got into a terrible row with a bloke he'd known for years.'

'That's how it happens,' said Gallagher sagely. 'And we *are* heading into show season, remember. Tensions can run pretty high.'

'Do you know,' said Harris thoughtfully, 'I am beginning to think you may be right, Matty lad.'

The sergeant looked pleased.

'You are?' he said.

'Yes, I am. Suddenly I can understand why someone might want to stick a nail through an allotment holder's head.'

Gallagher grinned and held up his hands.

'OK, OK,' he said. 'I promise to shut up about gardening.'

'Good idea,' said Harris. 'Right, our top priority is to confirm that this really is Michael Hills so see if you can track down the editor of the Herald, will you? I think he's called Gerrard. Show him the picture on the union card. He's bound to recognise him.'

'Yeah, will do,' said Gallagher. 'What are you going to do?'

'I'll stay around here for a while then I think that a visit to the vicar is in order. I suspect that we've strayed into his specialist subject.'

'Make sure you take your tambourine then,' said the sergeant. 'From what I hear about Jim Miles, you'll need it. Kumbaya and all that.'

* * *

The headlights cut through the darkness as the car edged its way along the rough hillside track leading to the old farmhouse, which sat halfway up a hillside off the main valley road outside Levton Bridge. As the vehicle entered the yard, the door of the house swung open to reveal a

13

young couple silhouetted by the light streaming from the hallway.

'Welcome to the Lighting the Way Faith Centre,' said David Fulton with a broad smile on his face as the driver got out of the car. 'How can we help you, friend?'

'Do you take confessions?' asked the driver.

He moved round to stand in front of the headlights so that his face was obscured by shadow but David Fulton did not need to see the features to know the identity of the speaker. He knew exactly who he was. Recognised the voice. Knew the long coat and the shiny black boots. Knew why he was here. David Fulton had been expecting his arrival for months. Secretly dreading his arrival for months, if he was honest; not that he had allowed the others to see his unease. Thomas Oldroyd was unfinished business.

'How did you find us?' asked David, trying to keep his voice steady.

'Not difficult to eavesdrop on your private little group chat.' Oldroyd stepped forward so that the couple could see the half-smile on his face. 'So, you still don't do confessions then?'

'No, but you are most welcome to come in. None of us wanted it to end as it did. If you wish to unburden yourself, you are most welcome to come inside and …'

'Only if you can absolve me from sin, David.'

'You know I cannot do that, Thomas. Only he has the power to absolve you for what you did. It is between you and him. However, we can pray together.'

Thomas snorted.

'Prayer is a mighty powerful thing,' said David. 'You should not under-estimate its power. Maybe it will help you find peace.'

'I believe in much more than prayer. You know that, David.'

'Nevertheless, our way remains the way of peace, Thomas, the path set out before us by a kind and loving

God,' said David. He sought the inner strength to banish his fear as Oldroyd stared at him with a strange look on his face. 'That will not change whatever you say or do.'

'You should read the Old Testament again,' said Oldroyd. He walked back round to the driver's door.

'Don't go,' said David, taking a step forward. He noticed that there was a shadowy figure sitting in the passenger seat. 'Who's your friend?"

'No one you know, David. Talking of friends, you'll never guess who I bumped into tonight in the town. John Halstead. And I thought he was dead. Strange old world, eh?'

Thomas Oldroyd swung himself into the car and started the engine.

'I'll see you around,' he said.

Oldroyd guided the vehicle back down the track. David and his wife walked to the edge of the yard and watched in silence as the lights of the car picked their way down the hillside and onto the valley road where they headed away from Levton Bridge and vanished into the darkness, the sound of the vehicle's engine gradually fading into the night.

'I hoped he would stay away,' said Judith quietly as they walked back to the house.

'We knew he would find us one day.'

'He scares me, David. Why do you think he mentioned John? Do you think he might have harmed him? He should have been here by now.'

'We must not think like that,' said her husband. 'We must not judge people. We must reach out to even the most troubled souls.'

'Not him, David.'

'Everyone. We must reach out to everyone, Judith.'

The couple walked back into the house and headed for the living room with its flickering coal fire and welcoming soft light cast by a lamp on the corner table.

'Do you think he had something to do with the theft of the bikes last night?' asked Judith. She walked over to the window and parted the curtains so that she could see into the yard. 'Do you think he's trying to frighten us again?'

'He sounded more like he wanted to unburden himself about something more serious than bikes.' David crouched down to stoke the fire with the poker. The embers sputtered into renewed life. 'If only he'd stayed. Perhaps we could have helped him. He is a man with demons is Thomas Oldroyd.'

'I'll lock the front door,' said Judith, leaving the room. 'We don't want them in here.'

Her husband followed her into the hallway, catching her up as she reached the door.

'We always said that we would not do that,' he said quietly. He reached out to take hold of her outstretched arm. 'We agreed that the house of the Lord should never close its doors to those in need. The parishioners at St Cuthbert's may think like that, but we don't. It is not our way.'

'That was before someone stole our bikes.' She shrugged off his hand and reached for the door key in the lock. 'And before Thomas Oldroyd and his friend turned up. You know what he's like, David. You saw what he tried to do to John last time.'

'Yes, but we must not…'

'I don't feel safe anymore.' She was close to tears. 'Perhaps coming here was a mistake.'

'The Lord will protect us.'

'He won't fit padlocks, will he, though?' she exclaimed. 'And what if they don't stop at bikes next time? You heard the detective this morning – she said we should be more security-conscious. We're not the only ones who have been targeted. And now we know that Thomas Oldroyd has found us…'

Before David could reply, a young, long-haired man walked down the stairs, followed by a short-haired girl in a patterned dress. She was no older than eighteen. The old timbers creaked when the couple reached the bottom of the stairs.

'What's happening?' asked Neil Harker. 'Who was in the car?'

'Strangers on the road seeking the blessed shelter of the Lord,' said David.

'Did you not invite them in?'

'Of course, I did,' said David. 'I offered to pray with them, but they drove away.'

'It was Thomas Oldroyd,' said Judith.

The two young people looked worried. Judith turned the key firmly in the front door.

'What did he want?' asked the girl anxiously.

'The usual,' said Judith. 'To cause trouble. I'm not taking any risks. That detective was right. We're very vulnerable up here.'

'The Lord will protect us if we only trust in him,' said David. He reached across her and turned the key back. 'He will protect us from everything.'

'Amen to that,' said Neil Harker.

But the fear behind his eyes suggested that he did not mean it. Like all of them, he had seen the fury that lurked deep within Thomas Oldroyd.

* * *

After leaving the church, Dennis McGuffin took a walk around the park in Levton Bridge. Usually, a man rooted deep in his convictions, he was surprised by the extent to which the confrontation with the young people had disturbed him, and McGuffin felt the need to calm the turbulent thoughts which had tipped the balance of his mind. Eventually, feeling more relaxed and as confident as ever that he had done the right thing in banishing them from St Cuthbert's, he walked to nearby Market Place and stopped at the Co-op to buy a bottle of wine. Dennis McGuffin did not drink much, had hardly touched a drop since the death of his wife from leukaemia the previous year, but tonight he felt the old cravings.

Still deep in thought and clutching his bottle of red, McGuffin walked slowly through the darkened streets for five minutes until he turned into a new housing estate. A couple of minutes later, he arrived at a three-bedroomed detached house, walked past the silver BMW parked on the drive and approached the front door. Which was when he noticed that the living room curtains had been drawn closed. McGuffin frowned; he was convinced that he had left them open when he left for the meeting at the church.

Shaking his head – he had been forgetting things more and more since his wife died – he turned the key in the front door and walked into the hallway, sighing as he always did as he was struck by how empty the house felt. McGuffin walked into the living room, flicked on the light and gasped as the illumination revealed a man sitting in one of the armchairs.

'Who the hell are you?' exclaimed McGuffin.

'Someone who knows what you did to Elaine Murphy,' said the man, whose quiet, measured tones masked menace. 'You cannot run for ever, Dennis. The day of reckoning has come.'

'I had nothing to do with Elaine Murphy's death! You ask the police.'

'The police may believe that you are innocent,' said the man, holding up his hand to reveal a knife, 'but I don't. And neither do the others.'

McGuffin stared at the blade, gave a slight gasp and dropped the bottle, which smashed on the edge of the coffee table and spilled its contents to create a crimson pool on the white carpet.

Chapter three

It took Gallagher and Butterfield thirty minutes to drive from Levton Bridge to Roxham at the bottom of the valley. The detectives travelled in silence as the sergeant guided his car down the dark and winding road, each officer wrapped in morbid thoughts after witnessing the crucifixion. Eventually, to their relief, the car reached the bright lights of the area's main town.

Parking in Roxham's deserted High Street, the officers walked over to the offices of the Herald, which were sandwiched between a newsagent's and a mini-mart. Standing outside was a bespectacled, short-haired man in his thirties, wearing jeans and a black T-shirt beneath his overcoat. He flapped a hand in greeting as the officers crossed the road towards him.

'Tony Gerrard?' said Gallagher.

'The very same.'

'Thanks for coming out,' said the sergeant as they shook hands. 'This is Detective Constable Butterfield.'

'Two of you, I'm honoured,' said the editor. He gave the warrant cards proffered by the officers a cursory glance and let them into the building. 'And intrigued. Methinks you have a good story for me.'

'All in good time, Mr Gerrard,' said Gallagher.

Flicking on lights as he went, Tony Gerrard led them through the reception area and through a rear door into a cramped newsroom with several desks cluttered with piles of papers.

'Grab a seat,' he said. Gerrard walked over to a small kitchen area at the end of the office. 'If you can find one. Cuppa?'

'That would be great,' said Gallagher, sitting down at one of the desks. 'How long have you been the editor?'

'Just over six months now. I was Deputy Chief Reporter at the Leicester Standard before that. It's another weekly paper.'

'Bit of a leap to editor.'

'They weren't exactly smashing the door down to be editor of the Roxham Herald,' said Gerrard. 'When the Group advertised it internally, I was the only one who applied. We're hardly Fleet Street here.'

Gerrard switched on the kettle and busied himself with the mugs.

'Besides,' he said, 'the move suited us. My missus had wanted to come home to be near her folks for ages. They're getting on a bit.'

'Same thing with my wife,' said Gallagher. 'We were in London. I was with the Met, but she missed home.'

'She got a job round here then?'

'Julie's a nurse at Roxham General. In fact, you used a picture of her on the front page a couple of months ago. The nurses on her ward did the half-marathon to raise money for a new scanner. She was the one dressed as a fox.' Gallagher chuckled. 'You called her Foxy Lady. She loved that, did Julie.'

'Yeah, I remember. Not exactly original but one of my better headlines nevertheless. She was standing next to a kangaroo and a tiger, if I recall correctly. Better than another sodding sheep on the front page, I guess.' Gerrard turned round from his tea-making, caddy in hand. 'Do you not find the valley a bit quiet after London?'

'Sometimes.' Gallagher noted Butterfield's expression. 'OK, yeah, most of the time.'

'But you wouldn't know it,' said Butterfield. 'He never mentions it.'

She instantly regretted the comment as the sergeant frowned; he was always telling her to think before she spoke, particularly when members of the public were present. Always present a united front was his constant mantra. You never knew if these things would come back to bite you. The constable inwardly cursed herself and looked down at the desk. Gallagher gave a half-smile but said nothing; she'd learn.

'Yeah, I miss Leicester,' said Gerrard. He had turned back to his tea-making and did not appear to have noticed the constable's reaction. 'Still, an editorship is something you have to take when it's on offer, even if it is only the Roxham Herald. And it worked out OK because Anne got a part-time job running the office at St Cuthbert's Church. You told our reporter on the phone that it was important?'

'I was surprised that anyone answered this time of night,' said Gallagher.

'She'd been covering a late council meeting. Three hours of windbags banging on about grass verges and dustbins. Still, it fills space, I suppose. So how can I help?' Gerrard turned round again, his eyes gleaming. 'Something big cracking off? You going to give me an exclusive, Sergeant?'

'We've had a murder at Levton Bridge.'

'That's bad timing.'

'What?'

'This week's paper went to print this afternoon, and we could have done with a good story.' Gerrard poured the hot water into the mugs. 'As it is, we're leading the front page on some twaddle about closing the public toilets in Market Place. I wanted to run it with the headline "Councillors Take the Piss" but it's not exactly our style.'

'I'm sure most folks would much rather read about that than a murder in the town.'

'You know that's not true.' There was a clinking sound as the editor stirred the tea. 'The punters love a good crime story, the gorier the better, as long as it hasn't happened to them. Is this one gory?'

'You could say that.'

'You going to tell me what happened?'

'Not at this stage.'

'Then why are you here?' Gerrard carried the mugs across, struggling as one of them started to slip from his grasp until the sergeant rescued it. 'Thank you. Disaster averted. From what I know of your DCI Harris, a journalist is the last person he'd want you to talk to. You going to at least tell me who the victim is?'

'I'm sorry to break this to you, Mr Gerrard, but we think that he is one of your reporters.'

'I can tell you now that he's not.'

'We think he might be, I am afraid. Trouble is, we can't seem to find any record of him so we thought you might be able to help.'

'Not unless he's had a sex change, I can't,' said Gerrard, taking a sip of tea. 'I've got three reporters and one sub-editor, and they're all women. As is our ad rep and the receptionist, for that matter. I'm the only man.'

'So, who's Michael Hills then?' asked Gallagher. He took the plastic bag containing the union card from his jacket pocket and held it up so that the editor could see the picture.

'He's no one,' said Gerrard, glancing at the picture.

'What do you mean, he's no one?'

'It's a house name, Sergeant. A lot of newspapers use them when they take copy from freelances or journalists who are employed elsewhere but are selling stories on the side. We've used them for years.'

'So, Michael Hills does not exist?'

'No, it's a made-up name. We've got two of them, in fact. Michael Hills for general news and features, particularly agricultural stuff.' He shuddered. 'He's very good on sheep insemination is Michael. The other name is Andrew Valli for the odd sport story. The surnames are in-jokes, apparently.'

'And you don't recognise the face?' asked Butterfield. She gestured to the card in Gallagher's hand.

'Sorry, no.'

'How many people use the name Michael Hills?' asked Butterfield, taking a sip of her drink.

'Only two.' Gerrard gave a rueful smile. 'I've not got much of a budget to buy stuff in, unfortunately, Constable. I'm lucky they let me spend that.'

'But our dead guy must have links with your newspaper if he knows about the name Michael Hills, surely?' said Gallagher.

'I'd be surprised if it was either of the two guys we use. One's an old boy over at Helwith who writes the occasional village news piece but doesn't want the benefits people to know, and the other fellow is employed by one of the big farming magazines but slips us the odd story for beer money. He says it's ok as long as we rewrite it so that his boss does not recognise the copy. That's no problem; it's usually shite anyway.'

'And Andrew Valli? Who's he really?'

'A young sports reporter on another paper who lets us use his rugby reports if local teams are involved, for beer money. His editor would sack him if he knew what he's doing. He's a bit of a stickler for that kind of thing, apparently.'

'But none of them are the guy on the card?'

'I am afraid not,' said Gerrard.

'What about in the past? Other people who might have worked for you?' asked the sergeant. 'Could he be one of them?'

'Who knows?' Gerrard shot him a sly look. 'Tell you what, if you let me take a photocopy I can ask if anyone knows him.'

'And see his picture slapped all the front page? I don't think so.'

'Worth a try. Not sure I can really help then. Like I said, I've only been here a few months, and the Group that owns this place only took over at the start of the year. It was them who suggested it was time my predecessor retired.' Gerrard took a sip of tea. 'He'd been here twenty-nine years. Seems that folks never move on here. The vicar of St Cuthbert's had been here for thirty-six years before that new lad replaced him, apparently. He's from Leicester, too, oddly enough.'

'Right,' said Gallagher, who was more interested in trying not to think of a lifetime spent in the valley. While he knew that it was a distinct possibility, the idea appalled a man more suited to the hustle and bustle of a big city. 'I guess we know more than we did five minutes ago anyway. So, how come this Hills fellow was able to get hold of a union card if he's not real?'

'You'd have to ask them, Sergeant, but I'm sure your governor has told you that we journalists are a scurrilous bunch who'll stop at nothing to get what we want.'

Gallagher ignored the comment and shot Butterfield a quick look to ensure that she said nothing as well; neither of them needed Jack Harris to tell them not to trust journalists. The sergeant drained his mug and stood up.

'We'll need contact details for the two guys who are writing as Michael Hills,' he said. 'Just to make sure. And for your Head Office, see if they can help us get hold of records from the previous owner of the newspaper.'

'Sure.' Gerrard scrolled down the contacts list in his mobile phone and scribbled the numbers on a piece of paper, which he handed to the sergeant.

'Cheers,' said Gallagher.

'Before you go,' said Gerrard. 'The paper may have gone to print, but I can still get something on our website tonight even if you won't let me have the picture. Be nice to break a proper exclusive for once. Sure, you can't tell me more about the murder?'

'I am afraid not,' said Gallagher. He gave the journalist a hard look. 'And I don't want you naming Michael Hills either. This conversation has been off the record. If you report any of it, I'll charge you with obstructing our inquiries.'

'There's nothing to stop me ringing the Duty Press Office, is there, though?'

'Knock yourself out, but I doubt they'll tell you anything tonight.' Gallagher headed for the door. 'We'll see ourselves out.'

The editor nodded and, as they left the room, had already switched on his computer and was reaching for one of the desk phones.

'I guess he's going to get his exclusive, after all,' said Butterfield as the detectives walked through reception.

'I guess.'

Once the officers were back on the street and heading for the car, Gallagher looked at the constable.

'So, who the hell is Michael Hills then?' he asked.

'I'm not sure,' said the constable, relieved that the sergeant had not mentioned her faux pas in the newsroom. 'One thing's for sure, Sarge, this is better than what I was working on.'

'Stolen bikes, wasn't it?'

'Yeah, three lots taken in the past week. Out-of-towners, as usual, I reckon. The last ones went from that kooky Christian fellowship place out near Bradby last night.' She hesitated. 'Look, I know it's a long shot, but I'm beginning to wonder if there may be a link with our dead man?'

'Not sure kooky Christians are into murder.'

'Nevertheless.'

'Yeah, may be worth checking them out.' The sergeant fished his car keys out of his pocket as they reached his vehicle. 'And I did hear that they'd been causing ructions at St Cuthbert's over recent weeks. They're a pretty fervent bunch, and it's not gone down well with the locals, apparently. How do you fancy communing with the Almighty before we call it a night?'

'You had better not let the governor hear you calling anyone else the Almighty.'

'Amen to that,' said Gallagher.

Chapter four

'So, what do you reckon, Doc?' asked Harris as he and the pathologist watched the dead man being taken down from the shed door by paramedics and placed in a body bag.

'I'll know more after the PM but there's nothing to suggest any other cause of death at the moment. You said local people heard him screaming?'

Harris nodded.

'Doesn't bear thinking about,' said the pathologist. He shuddered as a chill breeze rippled the trees lining the end of the allotment. 'I've never seen anything quite so brutal in forty years doing this job. Have you?'

'Not in the police.'

'But you have seen something similar?'

'When I was in the army. In Kosovo.'

'What happened?'

'You don't want to know, Doc,' said Harris. 'Suffice to say that nothing surprises me about human beings anymore.'

'You're probably right; I don't want to know.' The pathologist looked at the body being loaded onto a stretcher and shook his head. 'This is probably enough to give me nightmares on its own.'

'Whisky, that's the answer. You still get the nightmares, but you don't care as much.'

The pathologist nodded; everyone had heard about Jack Harris and his evenings spent drinking alone in his cottage half way up the Dead Hill not far from Levton Bridge. People coped in different ways, thought the pathologist as he looked at the inspector, and not for the first time he wondered what else Jack Harris had seen during his time in the armed forces. He decided not to ask.

A young uniformed constable walked up the path.

'I'm sorry, sir,' he said to Harris. 'But there's a man at the main gate demanding to see you.'

Harris raised an eyebrow. 'Demanding?'

'It's Harry Osborne, sir. I have tried to get rid of him but he won't take no for an answer.'

'No, I bet he won't,' sighed Harris. 'OK, bring him in – and don't stand on his bloody onions.'

'Sergeant Gallagher says it's too late in the season for…' the constable stopped speaking when he saw the inspector's expression. 'Sorry, sir. I'll go and get him.'

'You do that.' Harris watched as the constable walked gratefully down the path, relieved that he had not prompted one of the inspector's outbursts. The detective winked at the pathologist. 'I do so enjoy having a reputation, Doc.'

'You're a mischievous man, Hawk. Anyway, I'll leave you to it.' The pathologist started walking back down the path. 'I know Harry Osborne of old and I have no desire to listen to him wittering on. I'll let you know when I've got more.'

'Cheers, Doc.'

Harris watched gloomily as the pathologist left the allotment, standing aside to allow through the uniformed officer and a thin, grey-haired man in his sixties. After he had passed them, the pathologist turned, grinned and gave Harris a thumbs-up. The inspector gave a slight smile which was wiped away when Harry Osborne jabbed a finger in his direction.

'Chief Inspector Harris,' said Osborne angrily, 'your officers are walking all over the site, trampling on the vegetables, and I demand that they stop. The allotment holders have spent many hours looking after their plants and with show seas…'

'This is a murder scene, Harry. My people will stop searching when I tell them to and not before, and if they have to stand on every bloody cabbage to do it, then that's what they'll do.'

Osborne was about to reply when he caught sight of the body on the stretcher. The sight seemed to dampen down his fury as he appreciated the gravity of the situation.

'Constable Butterfield said he was a man called Michael Hills?' he said after a few moments.

'Apparently, although we're not convinced that's his real name. Are you sure he's not on your list of tenants, Harry? Someone sub-letting perhaps?'

'Our rules,' said Osborne starchily, 'do not allow sub-letting. It's against the regulations, and we don't make an exception for anyone.'

'Well, last time I looked, it was against the law to commit murder but someone still did it.'

'Yes, well, I can assure you that all our tenants abide rigorously by the rules, Chief Inspector. This has nothing to do with the allotments, of that you can be sure.'

'Can you swear to that, Harry? There's no sign of forced entry at the main gate, so we are wondering if the killers had a key to the site.'

'I think not, Chief Inspector.'

'So, you know where every one of the keys is then?' asked Harris. 'None of them missing?'

'None of them are missing.' Osborne bridled at the suggestion. 'All the tenants sign for their keys and I know where every one of them is.'

'Then how did the killers get in, Harry? There's always people prepared to get round the rules, and I need to know if they had a key.'

Osborne hesitated.

'Well?' said Harris.

'I am afraid that some of our plot holders ignore our rule about keeping the gate locked at all times,' sighed Osborne.

'I thought they were all law-abiding?'

'We do our best, Chief Inspector. We are very hot on security. That's why we had the perimeter fence put up in the first place. We'd had a couple of shed break-ins.'

'Was this plot one of them?'

'No, they were both down the other end. Your lot never caught who did it. I did complain to your commander and he said he'd do something about it, but nothing happened. Frankly, we were disgusted at the police's lack of action. It's not good enough, not good enough at all, and I told Superintendent Curtis as much. What's more, you failed to even…'

Harris scowled as he listened to Osborne, while watching the body being wheeled down the path towards them. Noticing that Osborne looked ready to continue with his tirade, the inspector held up a hand, and the stretcher came to a halt. The detective reached down and unzipped the top of the body bag to reveal the dead man's contorted face.

'Are you sure you don't recognise him?' he asked.

Osborne gazed at the twisted features, the ugly gash in the forehead and the horror in the dead eyes, went pale and turned away. Harris zipped the bag up again and the body continued on its way.

'Sorry if that upset you,' said the inspector with a slight smile but both men knew that he didn't mean it. 'Now, you were saying?'

'How did he die?' asked Osborne quietly. 'That hole in his head…'

'I'd rather not say at this stage, Harry, but you can see why I want your help, can't you? Whoever did that is very dangerous and they're still at large. I am worried that other allotment holders may be at risk.'

'But why would anyone target us, Chief Inspector?' Osborne looked bewildered. 'We've done nothing to cause something like this.'

'Has there been any trouble on the allotments recently?'

'Trouble? What kind of trouble?'

'Between the tenants. Any fights? Disputes?'

'There's always the odd disagreement about boundary fences, encroaching weeds, that sort of thing. Usually when we send out our warning letters.'

'Letters?'

'Yes, telling them to put things right.' Osborne sounded defensive. 'Me and Dennis McGuffin do it. We have to make sure that they obey the rules.'

'But some people object?'

'Some do, but there's not been anything serious. Not to warrant something like this.'

'You'd be surprised, Harry. According to my sergeant, the police in Bermondsey investigated a murder caused by a disagreement over leeks.'

'That's the south, though,' said Osborne dismissively. 'We're a bit more sensible up here.'

'Well someone wasn't,' said Harris. He gestured to the body now being loaded into the ambulance parked on the narrow track running past the allotment. 'This is Dennis's plot, I think?'

'Yes, it is.'

'I'll have to have a word with him then. Will he be at home, do you think?'

'I'm not sure. I rang him after your Constable came round to see me but there was no answer and, when I went to see him, the house was in darkness and his car had gone.'

31

'Yeah, it was missing when a couple of our officers checked as well.' There was a gleam in the inspector's eye. 'I think I am right in saying that Dennis is a religious man, am I not?'

Harry Osborne looked at the gaping holes in the shed door and gave the inspector a sick look.

'I'm sure that Dennis has got nothing to do with this,' he said. 'This is a friendly place.'

* * *

At the other end of the site, over by the main gate, Detective Constable James Larch was gaining a very different impression of life on the allotments as he stood and talked to a slim man in his early thirties. The man had thinning hair and was wearing a black T-shirt and jeans.

'So, there's been a lot of bad blood between plot holders?' said the detective.

'There's always folks falling out on allotments,' said Danny Morton. 'It's the nature of the beast.'

'Falling out about what, for goodness' sake? Surely, all you're doing is growing a few vegetables?'

'You'd be surprised, Constable. Anyway, it's not usually trouble between plot-holders. With this place, the trouble normally involves the committee. Them and their bloody letters.'

'Letters?'

'Yeah, from Harry Osborne. Him and that officious twat McGuffin. They have caused a lot of ill-feeling.'

Larch looked even more interested.

'I take it we are talking about Dennis McGuffin?' he said. 'Where does he fit into this then?'

'He's chair of the Inspection Committee,' said Morton. 'Every three months, him and his little pals do a tour of the site with their clipboards then Osborne and McGuffin send out heavy-handed letters to plot holders based on what they find.'

'Heavy-handed?'

'Yeah, they usually threaten to terminate your tenancy if you don't do as they say.' Morton sighed. 'Drains all the joy out of it sometimes. I've been thinking about quitting for a while. I don't need that shit. I get enough of that at work.'

'You got sent one then?' said the detective.

'I reckon everyone has.' Morton gave a mirthless laugh. 'Unless you're on the committee, of course. Perfect, they are. I've only been here two years and I've already received three. The last one was because McGuffin said that a pile of bricks next to my water butt was unsightly. It's all petty stuff. There's some small-minded people in this town.'

'So, it would seem.' Larch made a note in his pocketbook. 'Anyone ever take it further? You, for example?'

'What, like murdering one of them?' Morton gave a half smile. 'I dare say some of the tenants were tempted. Me? I ignore the letters. Neither Osborne or McGuffin have the balls to actually kick anyone off. Typical bullies. They back down the moment anyone stands up to them.'

'And someone has?'

Morton hesitated, alerted by the edge in the detective's tone of voice.

'It was nothing,' he said.

'Nevertheless.'

'OK, I did hear that one or two of the plot-holders had words with Dennis McGuffin after receiving the latest round of letters. One of them got pretty angry, from what I heard.'

'Who was it?'

'I don't mean to drop anyone in it.'

'I do need a name.'

'Henry Grace.' Morton gestured up the path. 'He's got the plot with the wonky trellis. I heard they had a furious set-to about it. Look, I don't want to get involved in this, you won't tell folks about what I just said, will you?'

'I'll do what I can,' said Larch.

Chapter five

'This is very troubling,' said the Reverend Jim Miles as he poured tea into bone china cups and handed one of them to Harris. 'Very troubling indeed.'

'You are the master of under-statement,' said the inspector.

It was shortly before 10pm, and the two men were sitting in the tidy living room of the Manse, a detached Victorian house standing in wooded gardens next to St Cuthbert's Church. Harris took a sip of his drink and reached for a biscuit from the glass coffee table. He glanced around at the religious paintings hanging on the walls; romantic images depicting shafts of light from Heaven and a smiling Jesus with arms outstretched to his followers. *Our worlds could not be more different*, thought Harris. And yet...

'However,' said the vicar, 'I am not sure I can really help you with your investigation.'

'It's a very specific crime,' said the inspector. He gestured to a large silver cross standing on a side table. 'Difficult to escape the Christian motif in the way he died, I would suggest, Jim.'

'I am struggling to come to terms with it,' said the vicar with a shake of the head.

'Not quite what you expected when you moved to sleepy old Levton Bridge, I imagine.'

'It has certainly been a more testing time than I envisaged.' The vicar looked even more troubled. 'Theological college is all very good at the theory, Chief Inspector, but they don't prepare you for real life. After what you have just told me, how on earth could they?'

The clergyman fell silent for a few moments and stared gloomily into the flickering flames of the fire in the grate. Jim Miles had only been in the parish for six months; it had been his first posting since giving up a career with an engineering company in Leicester to train for a new life in the clergy several years previously. Most of his time since arriving at Levton Bridge had been spent trying to develop relationships with the people of the valley but he had found the task more difficult than he had imagined. Even though most of them were not part of his dwindling congregation, they still viewed the new vicar with suspicion, partly because, he surmised, hailing from the East Midlands he was not a northerner and partly because he had replaced a clergyman who had served for many years at St Cuthbert's before finally retiring.

And now this, thought the clergyman as he stared at the dancing shadows in the flames; it all felt like a challenge too many. The events at the church earlier in the evening had shaken Jim Miles badly and the news just delivered by Harris had rendered him close to tears. Not for the first time in recent weeks, the clergyman felt the tears welling up deep inside and his faith wavering.

Harris, whose faith in his own abilities rarely, if ever, wavered sat and drank his tea as he allowed the clergyman time to compose his thoughts. The inspector, who had never been a religious man, had had few dealings with the vicar since his arrival but had heard that his evangelical ways had not gone down well with his largely traditional congregation. Now, the inspector sensed that Miles needed to unburden himself of deep concerns, so Harris gave the vicar time to compose his thoughts. The inspector never tired of extracting secrets from people.

'Any idea who your dead man is?' asked the vicar eventually. He broke away from the spell cast by the flames and looked at the detective. 'Do you have a name for him?'

Harris took a photocopy of the NUJ card from his jacket pocket and showed it to the vicar.

'That's him,' he said.

Was there, Harris asked himself, just the merest flicker of recognition? He could not be sure.

'I am sorry,' said the vicar, 'I have never seen him before.'

'Sure?'

'Sure, Chief Inspector. I don't recognise him.'

'No one does. The name on the card says he is called Michael Hills and it claims that he's a journalist.'

'The guy from the Herald?'

'You know him?'

'Just recognised the name. He writes a lot of stuff about sheep. Not my bag really but I have learned to take notice of such things since I came here.' The clergyman gave a slight smile. 'Are my parishioners not my flock? Although, from what I have seen of the way sheep behave, they are much easier to control than parishioners.'

'I suspect it's because they are more stupid.'

'Are we talking about sheep or parishioners, Chief Inspector?'

'I'll let you work that out for yourself.'

Harris waited for the vicar to reply but instead, the clergyman lapsed back into morose silence and stared into the fire again.

'Anyway,' said Harris, 'my sergeant has just rung to say that the editor of the Herald has confirmed that it's a fake name so we still have no idea who our dead man is. Rather hoped you might be able to help.'

'Why? Someone gets crucified, and you thought of me? Is that it?'

'Something like that. Call it spiritual guidance.'

'Crucifixion is not something the church encourages, Chief Inspector. Bring and buy sales, cake-making, yes; crucifixions, no. I don't know if you heard, but we've had some bad experiences with them in the past.'

Harris looked at the vicar for a few moments, trying to work out if he was joking; Jim Miles had always struck him as an earnest man who was not given to humour. The clergyman noticed the look.

'I'm sorry,' he said. 'That was in extremely bad taste. It's been a long day.'

'It certainly has. So, you've got no one in your congregation with the name Hills then?' Harris slipped the picture back into his pocket.

'I am afraid not.'

'Any trouble at the church?'

'Trouble?' asked the vicar quickly. 'Why would there be trouble?'

Harris noted a defensive tone in the clergyman's voice.

'I wondered if there had been any tensions?' he said. 'With the people from Lighting the Way, for example?'

The vicar felt the tears welling up again, fumbled in his cardigan pocket for a handkerchief and dabbed his eyes.

'You've heard about tonight then?' he said quietly, his voice shaking slightly with the emotion.

'All I've heard is the odd snippet over recent weeks. Words exchanged. Differences of opinion. What happened tonight?'

'It all came to a head,' said Miles. He spoke in a low voice, even though they were alone in the room apart from a cat dozing on the radiator. 'It was very unpleasant, and I cannot say I agree with what they did.'

'What came to a head? Who are they and what did they do?'

'I'm sure it's got nothing to do with your murder.'

'Nevertheless, it may be of interest.'

'Lighting the Way have given me a lot of trouble,' said the vicar sadly. He dabbed his eyes with the handkerchief again. 'The congregation think I'm far too evangelical for a place like Levton Bridge as it is but Lighting the Way, they're even more extreme in my parishioners' eyes. Let's just say that the locals are very set in their ways.'

Harris nodded. He knew the truth of the vicar's comment only too well from personal experience. Having grown up in Levton Bridge, a teenaged Harris had escaped the claustrophobia of the valley by joining the army after his rebellious nature had taken him into bad company, eventually leading to confrontations with older local people and warnings from the police. He had not returned to live in the area for many years and only then after leaving the army to work as a police officer in Manchester. Harris knew that he would return to Levton Bridge one day – he had always felt the pull of the northern hills – but he did so mindful of the drawbacks. Drawbacks that he sensed the Reverend Jim Miles had not thought through when he arrived to pursue his ministry in Levton Bridge.

'I imagine Lighting the Way was a shock to the system,' said the inspector.

'That's putting it mildly. You can probably guess what it was like when they pitched up to Sunday service one morning. Four of them, out of the blue and much younger than most of the parishioners. The congregation hated everything about them right from the off.'

'What exactly are Lighting the Way, Jim?' asked Harris. 'I have to confess that I'd never heard of them until they turned up here.'

'I'm not surprised. There's not many of them, and they are all rather fragmented. They started out in the East Midlands. They're a breakaway ecumenical group who want to shake the traditional church out of what they see as its staid ways. They have been looking for somewhere to create a centre of pilgrimage.'

'And they chose Levton Bridge?' Harris could not keep the disbelief out of his voice.

'It was something about the peace of the hills, I believe. They felt closer to God here than in Leicester.'

'That I can believe.' Harris thought of long days spent hiking across the tops with the dogs ambling in his wake. 'But they caused trouble instead?'

'I'm not sure they set out to do so.' The vicar sighed. 'It's just that the congregation at St Cuthbert's does not hold with shouting out loud in services when the spirit moves you and holding up your hands during prayer. The congregation likes things more traditional. Less, how can I say it, joyous?'

'Perish the thought that services should be joyous, Jim. What happened to a universal church open to all?'

'It's a good question and one with which I have been wrestling ever since I arrived in Levton Bridge. Do you know that I was second choice for the job? The Diocese felt it was time that the parish moved with the times, so they wanted to bring in a female vicar.'

'That would not have gone down well,' said Harris.

'How true,' said the vicar with a wan smile. 'Anyway, the congregation refused so they got me instead. Not that they see me as much better. Whenever I try to change anything, even something small, it's like the Devil is striding among them.'

Harris thought of the body nailed to the shed door.

'Perhaps he is,' he said with a wry smile.

'This not something to make jokes about, Chief Inspector.'

'Who's making jokes?' said Harris. 'So, what happened tonight to make things worse, Jim?'

'The congregation banned them.' The vicar looked at the detective with hooded eyes. 'Between you and me, my faith has been severely tested since I moved here, Chief Inspector. As you will have gathered, I am not entirely unsympathetic to the beliefs of Lighting the Way, but I find that I have to be careful what I say. Especially in front of people with such entrenched views.'

'You don't have to be careful in front of me. I got kicked out of Sunday school at this place for fighting when I was six. So, what exactly do Lighting the Way believe that's causing all the trouble?'

'That with true faith, anything is possible.'

'Surely, that's what you say every Sunday from the pulpit?'

'I know, I know,' sighed Miles. 'But there are limits.'

'I didn't think the Christian faith did limits,' said Harris, taking a sip of tea.

'Well, it does. Tonight's meeting was supposed to resolve things.' The vicar seemed close to tears again. 'I can't help feel we have failed the young people. What's worse, the congregation blame me for bringing them here. I had nothing to do with it but you try telling that to Dennis McGuffin. He won't have it.'

Harris looked at him sharply.

'What's he got to do with it?' he asked.

'Dennis is the one who banned them from the church tonight. He chairs the Parochial Church Council. It can sometimes be difficult to work out where the true evil lies.' The clergyman reached for the teapot. 'Top up?'

'Sure,' said Harris. 'That'll solve everything.'

* * *

The silver BMW pulled into a deserted lay-by on the quiet country road that led to the junction with the southbound M6, and the driver cut its headlights. He sat in silence for a few moments as he watched a second car pull off the road and park behind him. When its lights were extinguished, the lay-by was plunged into darkness and the driver of the BMW reached into the glove compartment and took out a torch. He got out of the vehicle and opened the boot, staring down into the face of a man whose wide eyes were illuminated by the beam of the flashlight, and whose terrified cries were muffled by the tape across his mouth.

'Let's get him out of sight,' said the BMW driver as he was joined by his accomplice, who had slipped a bag over his shoulders.

Together, they carried the struggling man into the nearby copse, the driver illuminating the way between the trees with his torch, the metallic items in the bag making a clinking sound. Once they judged that they were deep enough into the woodland to be sure that no one could see them from the road, the driver threw Dennis McGuffin to the ground and reached down to rip the tape from his mouth with a rough action that brought forth a pained shriek from the prisoner.

'Shut it!' snarled the accomplice.

He slammed a metal-tipped boot twice into his ribs. Engulfed by waves of pain and desperately fighting back nausea, McGuffin tried to scrabble to his feet but a third kick to the face sent him crashing to his knees where he stayed for a few moments, spitting out bile and fragments of tooth.

'That's for Elaine,' snarled the driver.

'I told you,' bleated McGuffin, cowering lest another blow be delivered. 'I had nothing to do with her death. I told you that and the police agreed that I...'

His voice tailed off as he watched the accomplice slip his haversack off his shoulders and tip out the contents, a hammer and masonry nail, which glinted in the torchlight.

'Oh, God, no!' screamed McGuffin.

He was hauled to his feet, and the men ignored his pleas for mercy as they started about their grim work. Within seconds, the night air was filled with the sound of hammering and the agonised shrieks of their victim before once again it fell silent, and his attackers walked long and easy back towards the lay-by.

Chapter six

Its headlights cutting a swathe of light through the blackness, Gallagher's car picked its way up the rough hillside track and pulled into the farmyard, where the sergeant parked next to a battered white minibus. Getting out, the sergeant noticed that the side of the vehicle bore a series of fish motifs. The lights were still on in the farmhouse and, as the sergeant and Butterfield got out of the vehicle and walked towards the building, the front door swung open and they could see a young man silhouetted in the door-frame, staring silently in their direction.

'Who he?' asked Gallagher.

'He seems to be their leader,' replied Butterfield. 'Bloke called David Fulton. Be warned, Sarge, he's a prickly character. He could not get rid of me quickly enough when I came up this morning to talk about the stolen bikes.'

'Why?'

'Not sure.'

'Perhaps it's something to do with your unique way with people.'

'Hey, I was perfectly polite,' protested Butterfield. 'Besides, his wife liked me, I think. She's nice.'

David Fulton recognised Butterfield as the detectives neared the house.

'Constable,' he said. 'Isn't it a bit late to be making enquiries into stolen bicycles?'

'It's a bit more serious than that, I am afraid, Mr Fulton,' said Butterfield. 'This is Detective Sergeant Gallagher. Can we come in?'

'All are welcome here.' Fulton stood aside to let them in. 'We are all friends in the House of the Lord.'

'Right,' said Gallagher.

He stepped into the hallway and noticed hanging on the wall a large framed painting of Jesus standing on a hilltop; he was bathed in light and had his arms outstretched. The image meant nothing to Matty Gallagher. Although many people had commented on his likeness to a monk down the years, the sergeant was not a religious person and struggled to empathise with those who were.

A couple of minutes later, the detectives were sitting next to each other on the sofa in the small living room, cradling mugs of tea made by Judith Fulton. Dotted around the room in other chairs were the four members of Lighting the Way. Gallagher tried to size them up. Butterfield was right about David Fulton, he decided, definitely an awkward character, and his wife may well have been more amenable than her husband but now all the sergeant saw was tension, her eyes betraying anxiety. There was something about the appearance of the two others that he could not quite place. Then it came to him. Innocence. The teenagers were innocents; the thought struck a chord with a detective more used to dealing with criminals. And, for reasons he could not rationalise, the idea disturbed him.

'You said it was serious,' said David Fulton, looking at the detectives. 'Has something happened?'

'I am afraid so,' said Gallagher, breaking off from his reverie. 'A man was murdered in Levton Bridge earlier tonight.'

'I am not sure what it has got to do with us.'

'There's a religious motif to the crime, Mr Fulton. He was nailed to the door of a shed.'

'Dear God,' gasped Judith Fulton. She clapped a hand to her mouth.

The other two young people looked shocked. David Fulton, though, remained calm.

'Awful as that is,' he said. 'I still do not see why you are here.'

'You were burgled last night, I think?' said Gallagher.

'It's a big jump from stealing mountain bikes to nailing people to shed doors.'

'I accept that,' said the sergeant. 'But this is a quiet area so anything out of the ordinary is worthy of further investigation, especially when we have had a murder. Has anything else unusual happened apart from the break-in?'

Fulton shook his head.

'Nothing,' he said.

He shot a look at the others and they did not reply, but the worried expressions on their faces was not lost on Gallagher, hard as they tried to disguise them.

'Are you sure?' said the sergeant. He stared at each one of them in turn. 'Nothing at all? No unexpected visitors? Anything like that?'

They all shook their heads, apart from Judith, who glanced at her husband then looked away and stared into the fire.

'Nothing has happened, Sergeant,' said David Fulton.

'But…'

'Nothing.'

Gallagher noted the resolute expression on David Fulton's face and nodded.

'OK,' he said and reached into his coat pocket and produced the photocopied picture of Michael Hills. 'Do you know this man?'

He held it up so that they could all see in the low light cast by the table lamps. For a moment, the sergeant thought that Judith was about to speak but she glanced at her husband again, seemed to think better of it and remained silent. Fulton shook his head, and the other two said nothing.

'I have never seen him,' said David. 'None of us have. Is he the poor unfortunate person who was murdered?'

'He is. He goes by the name Michael Hills but we believe it's a fake name. He seems to be masquerading as a journalist.'

'Well, we don't know him,' repeated David, more forcefully this time. 'However, we will pray for his soul, of that you can be sure. Is there anything else, Sergeant? It is rather late.'

'You've been causing waves at St Cuthbert's, I understand? A bit of a bust-up tonight, from what I hear.'

'There was a disagreement, yes, but I fail to see what that has to do with your murder,' said Fulton.

'What was the disagreement about?'

'The congregation does not appreciate the way we worship.' Fulton looked knowingly at the sergeant. 'People tend to react negatively to things they do not understand. I am sure you can appreciate that.'

'And the people at the church…'

'I do not wish to talk about what happened tonight.' Fulton looked at the others. 'None of us do.'

Gallagher stood up.

'OK, so be it,' said the sergeant. He walked into the hallway. 'But you know where we are if anything occurs to you.'

Recovering from his own surprise at the speed of Gallagher's departure, David Fulton followed him.

'I am sorry that we have not been more helpful,' he said as he opened the front door to let the detectives out – but he did not sound sincere. 'However, as you can see, we live a quiet life of contemplation here. Not much happens.'

'I'm not sure that's quite true,' said Gallagher. 'According to my chief inspector, what actually happened tonight was that you got yourself banned from St Cuthbert's.'

'Change comes slowly to places like this. As a fellow outsider, you'll know that only too well. However, change *will* come to Levton Bridge if the Lord wishes it. A few narrow-minded bigots will not stop it happening.'

'Yes, well, good luck with that,' said Gallagher. 'Tell me, David, where were you before you came here?'

'I told you, it is late and…'

'Humour me.'

'Leicester,' said Fulton. 'We had a house on the edge of the city.'

'So, what brought you here then? It's a long way from the East Midlands.'

'We follow the Lord's bidding.'

'And he suggested that you up sticks and come to Bradby, did he?' said the sergeant. He was unable to keep the scepticism from his voice. 'This the Promised Land, is it? I've heard it called many things but never that.'

Although born and bred in the area, Butterfield allowed herself a slight smile. Everyone knew that Matty Gallagher had struggled to settle in the valley after life in London. For his part, Fulton bridled at the mockery in the detective's voice.

'We take our religion very seriously,' said Fulton. 'I'd thank you to afford us the same respect, Sergeant.'

'Sorry.' Gallagher's turn to sound insincere. He looked up the staircase into the darkness of the landing. 'Nice gaff. Do you own it?'

'We rent it. It's owned by a farmer who went into a home. He has dementia, I believe.'

'And does the Lord pay the rent?' asked the sergeant.

Fulton gave him an irritated look.

'He always provides his followers with what they need,' he said. Fulton opened the door wider as an invitation for the detectives to leave. 'I have to say that I find your cynicism somewhat offensive, Sergeant Gallagher. All you need is faith to make things happen.'

'Yes, well, I'll remember that the next time the bank asks why I am late on my mortgage payment,' said Gallagher.

He and Butterfield stepped out into the chill of the night. As they did so, a thought struck the sergeant and he turned back towards Fulton.

'Do you know a woman called Gerrard?' he asked. 'She was living in Leicester before she came here as well.'

'It's a big city, Sergeant.'

'Yes, but she works in the office at Cuthbert's now – Levton Bridge is a small town.'

'It certainly is. I may have seen her once or twice but only to look at. As you have so rightly observed, relationships were hardly cordial.'

'What about her husband then? Tony Gerrard? He was a journalist on the Leicester Standard, I think. Edits the Roxham Herald now.'

'We do not talk to journalists.' Fulton gave Gallagher a pointed look as the detectives stepped out into the gathering chill of the night. 'They tend not to be sympathetic to us – rather like police officers.'

Before the sergeant could reply, Fulton closed the door in the officers' faces. Gallagher raised an eyebrow at Butterfield, and the detectives headed back to the car. Once they were in the vehicle, Butterfield looked back towards the house and saw a sombre-faced Judith Fulton watching them through a gap in the living room window curtains. She stepped back out of view when she saw that she had been spotted by the detective.

'They're lying,' said the constable.

'In my experience,' said Gallagher, turning the key in the ignition, 'people usually are.'

'Do you not think we should go back in?' Butterfield kept staring at the house, but Judith Fulton did not reappear. 'Push them a bit harder? Did you see their expressions when you showed them the picture of Michael Hills? I reckon they know him.'

'Maybe they do.' Gallagher switched on the headlights. 'But I'm not sure it'll do us much good if we go back now. They didn't look in the mood to say anything, and you're right about David Fulton. Let's give them the night to chew things over.'

'Yes, but…'

'Look, they're just a bunch of well-meaning, but misguided, young people, if you ask me.' The sergeant steered the car out of the farmyard. 'A bit intense but nothing more. They're probably just spooked by having to talk to cops. Probably never done it before and now we turn up twice in a day. I still reckon the answer to the murder lies on those allotments.'

'Nevertheless, there's something not right.'

'We need to do a bit more digging before we come back – assuming we *do* come back. But I can't really see them having anything to do with the murder.' The sergeant noticed her crestfallen expression. 'Look, if it makes you feel better, that can be your first job in the morning. See what you can find out about them. Just don't waste too much time. Come on, let's get back to The Factory.'

Ignoring the constable's unhappy expression, Gallagher guided his car down the rough track, cursing as the headlights struggled to pick out the large stones that lay in the way.

'Bloody hell, it's like a scene from Fast and Furious,' he said. The sergeant tried to lighten the mood. 'I've always been told that I look like Vin Diesel. Oh, no, hang on, this car's a diesel, that's it.'

'You're one funny man,' said Butterfield but she did not sound amused.

The constable gripped the seat as the car careered round a bend in the track, the headlights picking out a row of swaying trees positioned closer to the vehicle than she would have liked.

'What do you think I should be looking for about Lighting the Way tomorrow?' she asked when the vehicle arrived at the road.

'You can start by finding out why they left the metropolitan delights of Leicester to set up in the arse-end of beyond.'

'Hey,' protested the constable. 'You're talking about the place where I was born and bred.'

'Then you know what I mean,' said the sergeant.

* * *

'It was just a few words uttered in the heat of the moment,' said Henry Grace as Detective Constable James Larch sat in at his kitchen table, cradling a mug of tea. They were in one of the terraced houses off Market Place, and it was shortly after 11pm. 'Nothing more than that. Why so interested in what I said to Dennis McGuffin anyway?'

'There was a murder on his plot tonight.'

'I didn't know that.' Grace sat in silence as he digested the information then shot the detective a worried expression. 'Is it Dennis?'

'No, but he seems to have gone missing and we would very much like to speak to him.'

'Surely you do not think that he committed the murder?'

'It's very early in our enquiries.' Larch took a photocopy of the picture of Michael Hills out of his pocket and showed it to Grace. 'Do you recognise this man?'

'I have never seen him before in my life.'

'You and everyone else.'

'Who is he?'

'The victim. He goes by the name Michael Hills but we think he may be called something else. So, back to Dennis McGuffin, Mr Grace, I take it you *did* fall out with him then?'

Henry Grace sighed.

'I am afraid to say that it did,' he said. 'I'm not proud of what happened, Constable, it was somewhat unseemly for a man of standing in the community, but I really don't see what's it got to do with your murder.'

'When it did happen?'

'Ten, eleven days ago. The start of the dry spell.' Grace took a sip of tea. 'I'd received the letter a couple of days before. McGuffin and his little pals objected to the state of my trellis. That's how petty they get. The letter said that I had a week to fix it or my tenancy would be terminated.'

'So, you decided to have it out with him?'

'Quite the opposite. I was going to ignore it like I did the other letters but that evening I went down to do some watering and bumped into McGuffin on one of the paths. I was going to walk past him. Maintain a dignified silence. Be the bigger man.'

'So why didn't you?'

'Something about the way he smirked at me set me off, and I lost it.' Grace shook his head. 'A man of my age yelling profanities like a bloody fishwife. Ridiculous! And before you ask, totally out of character, but he can be extremely infuriating can Dennis McGuffin.'

'So I am hearing,' said the constable, making a note in his pocketbook. 'He seems to be someone who evokes strong emotions in people.'

'He's a self-important tosspot, that's why. I'm not the only one who thinks that either. He's not exactly popular among the plot-holders.'

'What did he do when you shouted at him?'

'Just stood there with his mouth open. I'm not surprised, I hardly know the man and here I was yelling at him. Then he said I'd be kicked off the allotments and walked away.'

'And *have* you been kicked off?'

'No. The man's a typical bully. Same with Harry Osborne. They send their silly letters but the moment someone stands up to them they go to pieces. I've heard nothing more about it, nor do I expect to.'

'And that was all there was to it?' asked Larch. 'You didn't assault him or anything like that?'

Grace looked shocked at the suggestion.

'Of course not,' he said. 'My anger was gone as quickly as it came. Even as I was shouting at him, I realised how ridiculous it all was. I'm President of Rotary, for God's sake. Can I ask how you found out about this?'

Larch stood up and drunk the last of his tea.

'You can ask,' he said, heading for the door, 'but I'm not going to tell you. I may need to come back and take a formal statement at some stage.'

'Why?' Grace looked anxious. 'My foolish behaviour doesn't need to become public knowledge, does it? I have a reputation to think about and, like I told you, it's nothing to do with the murder.'

'Then you have nothing to worry about,' said Larch. He walked into the hallway. 'Oh, one more thing, I understand you were recently elected onto the church council at St Cuthbert's.'

'Yes, that's right.'

'Do you know anything about the bust-up involving Dennis and Lighting the Way earlier tonight?'

'I was there.'

'We are wondering if it might be connected with the murder.'

'It was nothing. Yes, it went a bit too far, Dennis doing what Dennis does, but I am sure there is no connection with your murder.'

'Nevertheless…'

'The Lighting the Way people may be many things, Constable, but murderers they are not. Whatever you might think of Christians, we are peaceable people.'

'I'll take your word for it,' said Larch. 'But I'm beginning to wonder.'

Out on the street a few minutes later, the detective constable got into his car and dialled Matty Gallagher's number on his mobile.

'Sarge,' he said when the call was answered, 'just ringing to say that you are right about allotment holders. They're all bloody crackers.'

'Ah, a prophet in his own land,' said Gallagher. 'Talking of prophets, you find out anything about what happened at the church?'

'Sounds like they had a few words but that's about as far as it went.'

'Fair enough,' said Gallagher.

* * *

After ringing the doorbell for a third time and receiving no reply, Jack Harris stepped back into the road and thoughtfully surveyed Dennis McGuffin's darkened house. He glanced at the two uniformed officers walking towards him.

'Anything round the back?' asked Harris.

'No, it all looks fine,' said one of the officers. 'I looked through the kitchen window, but there's nothing to suggest anything is wrong.'

'You get anywhere with the neighbours?'

'They reckon it's not unusual for him to be out late,' said the other officer. 'Apparently, he lost his wife last year – cancer – and he sometimes goes for a late-night drive if he can't sleep.'

'Anyone see him go tonight?'

'I am afraid not.' The officer gestured to a house on the other side of the road where the inspector could see a

54

white-haired woman trying to hide from view but failing to conceal her shadow through a net curtain in the front room window. 'She reckons he went out on foot about half six then she noticed that the car had gone when she got home from her daughter's about tenish.'

'But she didn't actually see him go out in it?'

'Nope. You want us to break in?'

'Yeah, go on.'

Five minutes later, Harris was standing in the living room staring down at the crimson red wine stain on the carpet.

'What do you think?' asked one of the uniformed officers. He came to stand next to the inspector. 'There's no sign of a struggle. He *could* just be out on a night drive.'

'He could be.'

'In which case, there'll be hell on when he gets back,' said the uniform. 'He's an awkward customer is Dennis McGuffin. He'll not appreciate us smashing his door in. You want us to hang around? In case he comes back?'

'Please.'

'He a suspect?'

'Not sure what he is,' replied Harris, looking again at the wine stain.

'He may be a pernickety bastard but he's not a killer.'

'And yet,' said Harris, thinking back to his conversation with the vicar, 'I was reminded earlier tonight that sometimes it can be difficult to work out where the true evil lies.'

Chapter seven

'So where are we with all of this?' asked Jack Harris. 'I would like some answers, and I'm not the only one. The media have been queuing up.'

'You can't move for journalists outside the allotments,' said Gallagher, who was sitting in the front row.

He looked at the chief inspector, who was standing in front of the other detectives in the briefing room at Levton Bridge Police Station. The mood was subdued; neither Harris nor his team had enjoyed much sleep since the discovery of the body. Dawn had broken more than an hour previously but the sky above the northern hills was still grey and gloomy, and the rain battered cold and hard against the window. The stark contrast to the balmy soft summer sun of the previous evening had created a sombre mood in the room. The inspector's dogs, Scoot and Archie, rescue animals of indeterminate breeds, were curled up asleep beneath a radiator in the corner of the room.

'Yeah, there's media everywhere,' said Butterfield, who was sitting next to the sergeant. 'There were at least four television vans when I passed by on my way in. One of them was French TV.'

'And I've got nothing to tell any of them,' said Harris wearily. 'OK, before we talk about the plot-holders, what about the happy clappies? Are we *really* saying they may be involved?'

'I can answer that one,' said a dark-haired woman sitting behind Gallagher. Gillian Roberts was Levton Bridge's detective inspector, a mother-of-two in her early fifties whose matronly demeanour masked a mind as sharp as they came. 'My friend Edie Prentice goes to St Cuthbert's, and she says Lighting the Way never shut up about love and peace. I can't see them being involved in a murder.'

'It's amazing how many acts of violence are committed in the name of peace,' said Gallagher.

'Yes, very philosophical, Matthew, but there's nothing to link them with what has happened, is there? I know they fell out with the folks at St Cuthbert's…'

'And Dennis McGuffin *is* still missing, remember,' said Gallagher.

'Yes, he is but forensics found nothing of interest at his house, did they? He could simply be away for the night. We could waste an awful lot of time on what happened last night at the church.'

'Maybe not.'

'What does that mean?'

'It seems that all is not harmonious in the world of love and peace,' said Gallagher with the satisfied expression of a magician preparing to pull a rabbit from a hat. 'Constable, would you do the honours, please?'

Butterfield went around the room handing out computer print-outs.

'What am I looking at?' asked Roberts. The detective inspector was unable to conceal her irritation at the smug look on the constable's face. Nor, given how tired she felt and how bad her headache was becoming, did she attempt to.

'This news item,' said Butterfield, 'appeared on the Leicester Standard newspaper website several months ago after police were called to a disturbance at a house rented by Lighting the Way. One man sustained cuts to his face.'

'Is he named?' asked Roberts, scanning the article, which appeared beneath a picture of a semi-detached 1930s house.

'Unfortunately, not.'

'Anyone charged?'

'There's no indication that anyone was even arrested,' replied Butterfield. 'It's the only story I can find, so I am guessing nothing happened. Leicester Police are ringing me back to make sure.'

'So, it's a one-off incident three hundred miles away from Levton Bridge,' said Roberts dismissively. 'Why on earth should we be interested?'

'Because,' said Gallagher, intervening as he noted Butterfield's irritation, 'if nothing else, it suggests that these people attract trouble wherever they go.'

'You're grasping at straws.' Roberts looked at Butterfield. 'You both are.'

'Hang on,' protested the constable, 'I still reckon they are worth looking at – whatever Edie Prentice says. I mean, she's hardly an authority on investigating murders, is she?'

'Nor, might I say, are you,' said Roberts tartly; she had long struggled with the brash young constable's ways. 'And I'll thank you to show more respect to a senior officer.'

'At least I know not to dismiss a lead out of hand,' said Butterfield. She held up the print out. 'What's more, I've just noticed the name of the reporter who wrote the piece. Tony Gerrard. He was on the Leicester Standard before he became editor of the Roxham Herald. Small world, eh?'

'It is,' said Harris before Roberts could respond. 'And in my experience, most murders happen in small worlds. You've spent the most time with them, Alison, what do you make of them?'

'They were certainly very evasive when we went to see them last night.' The constable looked at Gallagher. 'Like they were withholding information from us.'

'They were certainly a bit off,' said the sergeant. 'Especially their leader. A bloke called David Fulton. He couldn't get rid of us quickly enough.'

'OK,' said Harris, 'go back and see them again but they're not suspects so try to keep it amicable and low-key. The last thing I want is the media saying that we have hauled God's emissaries on earth in for questioning. You happy with that, Gillian?'

'Not sure happy is the word,' she said grudgingly. 'I still reckon there'll be an innocent explanation.'

'So, let's not rule out Matty's suggested link with the allotments either.' Harris looked at James Larch, who was sitting next to Gallagher. 'Anything from the plot holders?'

'Plenty,' said Larch. He looked at a group of uniformed officers sitting further along the same row then ran his finger down a piece of paper resting on his lap, mouth moving silently as he counted. 'We got to see twenty-three plot-holders last night, and we should get to the rest today. Suffice to say that Dennis McGuffin was not Mister Popular. It's amazing how much bad feeling there's been on those allotments. I mean, they're only growing a few crappy vegetables?'

'I'd rather you did not describe their vegetables as crappy,' said Gallagher.

A ripple of laughter ran round the room, diffusing the tension. Harris let it die out then looked again at Larch.

'Anyone stand out from your interviews?' asked the inspector.

'One, yes,' said Larch. 'Henry Grace. He's a retired accountant, had the office in Hillside Road. He had a big dust-up with Dennis McGuffin a few days ago.'

'That's not like Henry. He always struck me as a fairly mild character but bring him in if you think it's necessary. Why did they fall out?'

'McGuffin insulted his wonky trellis.'

'Crackers,' replied Harris with a shake of the head. 'They're all crackers.'

The inspector pointed a finger at Gallagher as the sergeant opened his mouth to speak.

'And you can keep your opinions to yourself,' he said.

Gallagher closed his mouth but everyone could see that he was enjoying the conversation. Everyone turned as a balding uniformed officer walked into the room. Philip Curtis, the Divisional Commander, glanced at the inspector's dogs slumbering beneath the radiator and frowned. Although he and Harris had worked hard to develop a good working relationship after a difficult few months following the superintendent's appointment, the presence of the dogs at the police station remained one of their disagreements. However, Curtis knew only too well that the animals were popular with the rest of the staff, so he made no comment.

'The press conference will be staged here at 10am,' he said instead. 'Do we have anything to tell them?'

'Not much, sir,' said Harris; he'd started using the word more and more as their relationship had improved. 'Our man's identity remains a mystery. No updates, I think, Matty lad?'

'Not really. The union says that the card's a forgery and their duty guy did not recognise the picture when I emailed it over. Oh, and we got hold of the two guys who use the Michael Hills pseudonym, but they're straight up.'

'I understand you're also looking at this religious bunch?' said Curtis.

'Among other people, yes,' replied Harris.

'Not sure I can see it,' said Curtis. 'My wife met them when Roxham Methodist Church visited St Cuthbert's for a service last month. She said they seemed pretty harmless. Just a bit serious.'

'The question,' said Harris, 'is are they serious enough to kill?'

* * *

The air in St Cuthbert's Church was cold and sharp as the Reverend Jim Miles knelt before the altar, his eyes closed, hands clasped together, lips moving in silent prayer and tears streaming down his cheeks. He had been there for the best part of an hour and, so intense was his concentration, that he did not hear the woman push her way in through a side door. Anne Gerrard stood and watched him in concerned silence for a few moments then walked across the stone floor, the click of her shoes reverberating in the still air of the church.

'Jim?' she said when he did not acknowledge her presence. 'Are you alright?'

It took him a few moments to respond, and when he looked at her, she saw that tears had stained grubby rivers down his face.

'Not really,' he said, standing up unsteadily. He fumbled in his waistcoat pocket for a handkerchief, with which he dabbed his eyes. 'I keep seeking guidance but all I hear is silence.'

'I am sure that he will speak to you when the time is right, love.'

'I wish I had your faith.'

'Faith is all. You know that.' She gave him a reassuring nod. 'He will not abandon you in your hour of need. He has never abandoned you yet, has he? Has he not always shone a light on the path you must take?'

'I suppose you are right.' The vicar sighed. 'I take it you've heard about the murder?'

'Yes, two detectives came to see Tony about it last night. The police thought at first that the dead man might be one of his journalists. Do you know who he is?'

The vicar hesitated, struggling to compose himself.

'It's John Halstead,' he said eventually.

'But he's dead,' she exclaimed, staring at him in horror.

'Well, he is now.'

'Are you sure about this?'

'I'm positive. DCI Harris showed me his picture last night.'

'He came to see you?'

'Just after you left last night. Harris said that they think the dead man is called Michael Hills but it was definitely John. I recognised him immediately.'

'Why did you not tell me this last night?' She looked hurt. 'I could have come back over.'

'I didn't want to worry you.'

'I'd rather have known, love,' she said. Anne reached out to gently touch his arm. 'We don't keep secrets from each other, that's what we agreed. We face everything together.'

'I know, I know. I wasn't thinking straight. What with the meeting then the shock of hearing about John, I didn't know what to do for the best.' He reached up to touch her hand. 'I'm sorry.'

'Did you tell Jack Harris that you knew who it was?'

'I thought it best not to. I don't want either of us to be involved in this unless we really have to be. It could get very messy, and we have to protect ourselves. We could both lose our jobs.'

'You're right, love.' She gave him a hard look. 'Are you sure you didn't know that John was still alive?'

'Of course, I didn't. I'd have told you if I had.'

'What do you think he was doing here?'

'Perhaps he wanted to make amends.'

'Maybe,' she said. 'I did wonder if it was Dennis McGuffin who had been murdered. I heard that he went missing after last night's meeting?'

'He did, yes, but it was definitely John Halstead.'

'Do they know how he was killed?'

The vicar turned dark eyes on her.

'He was crucified,' he said quietly. 'Nailed to a shed door.'

Anne Gerrard gasped and the colour drained from her cheeks. She was silent for a few moments.

'Do the police know who did it?' she asked eventually.

'I don't think they know much really.'

'So, they don't know about Thomas Oldroyd then?'

'Harris didn't mention him.' The vicar looked at her sharply. 'Why, what do you know?'

'Nothing, but don't tell me that you didn't think of him when you heard what had happened to John. You know what Thomas is like.'

'I did think of him, yes. It was the first thing I thought of, in fact.'

Anne was silent again.

'Does Jack Harris know about us?' she asked eventually.

'I don't think so. And I saw no reason to tell him.'

'Best keep it that way.' Anne reached up to run a finger down one of the rivers of tears that were coursing down his cheeks again. 'Like you say, it's best not to get involved.'

'I fear,' said the vicar, 'that it's too late for that.'

And he dabbed his eyes with his handkerchief.

* * *

'You want me to do what?' said Gillian Roberts in amazement.

She was sitting in the interview room just off main reception at Levton Bridge Police Station and staring across the table at her old friend Edie Prentice, who sat with her arms crossed as she stared defiantly at the detective inspector, fire in her eyes. The women had known each other for forty years, ever since Edie had babysat Gillian when she was a child, and the detective believed that she knew the pensioner well enough not to be surprised by anything she said. Now, though, Gillian Roberts was finding out just how wrong she had been.

'I want you to arrest those horrible people,' demanded Edie. 'David Fulton and the others, I want you to arrest them.'

'For what reason?'

'Dennis is missing, and I think that they had something to do with it.'

'What on earth makes you think that?' asked the detective inspector. 'We don't even know that he's come to any harm. There could be a perfectly innocent explanation. He could simply have gone away for the night.'

'He said nothing about going away, Gillian.'

'Why would he tell you if he was?'

'I'd have known.' Edie hesitated for a few moments. 'I suppose you'd find out eventually. We've become close since his wife died.'

'What, you and Dennis McGuffin!' exclaimed Roberts, unable to keep the incredulity out of her voice. She noticed how offended Edie looked. 'Sorry. I apologise. So, you didn't see him after the meeting then?'

'Dennis said that he needed some time on his own to think things through. He was very upset by the way David Fulton talked to him at the church last night. He was very rude to Dennis.'

'It's hardly a crime, Edie,' said Roberts. 'What's more, Dennis can rub people up the wrong way himself; you know that. He is hardly a shrinking violet.'

'Yes, I know, Gillian, but this thing with Lighting the Way has put him under a lot of stress and that's the last thing he needs since his wife died.'

'Yes, but…'

'He may look like a confident man on the outside but he's more fragile than people think, is Dennis. Lilian's death hit him hard and David Fulton and his friends have just made it worse. They're the people you should be arresting, Gillian. Not harassing respectable citizens like Henry Grace.'

'We have to…'

'What your people did was a disgrace. Henry's very upset. He told me all about it this morning. I had to put three sugars in his tea.'

'My, you have been busy,' murmured the detective inspector, glancing up at the wall clock, which read ten past nine.

'We look after each other up here; you know that, Gillian. This is a supportive community.'

'But not if you're someone like the people from Lighting the Way?'

'Them!' The word was spat out with a vehemence that started the detective. 'They're wicked!'

'That's a strong word, Edie. Besides, I thought you said they were peaceable?'

'Yes, well, I've changed my mind. If anything has happened to Dennis, it'll be down to David Fulton. There's something of the Devil about that man. They tried to take our church and all Dennis wanted to do was protect us.'

'But change can be a good thing, can't it?'

'You sound just like them,' snorted Edie. 'You talk to David Fulton, and you'll see. I only really saw him for what he truly was last night. Are you going to arrest him?'

'I'm sorry, Edie, but we don't think there is any reason to.'

'Then think again.' Edie stood up and walked to the door. As she reached for the handle, she turned to face the detective and jabbed a bony finger in her old friend's direction. 'Just you think again.'

It was a thoughtful Gillian Roberts who watched her old friend walk out of the room. When Edie had gone, an image flashed into the detective inspector's mind, Alison Butterfield's smug expression as she handed out the print out from the Leicester Standard website.

'No,' said Roberts with an emphatic shake of the head. 'No, no, no.'

Chapter eight

Butterfield and Gallagher were on their way out of the CID room when the detective constable's mobile phone rang. She fished the device out of her coat pocket and took the call.

'Alison Butterfield?' said a young woman's voice. 'Stella Gaunt from Leicester CID. I gather you want to talk to me about Ravensdale Road?'

'I do, yes, Stella. Thank you for ringing back.' Butterfield noticed Gallagher standing at the door. 'I'll catch you up, Sarge.'

He flapped a hand in her direction and disappeared into the corridor.

'So, how can I help you?' asked Stella Gaunt. 'Leicester's a long way from Levton Bridge or whatever they call it. Took me ages to find it on the map.'

'A lot of people have that problem, Stella. I'm interested in exactly what happened at Ravensdale Road. All I've got to go on is a report on the Leicester Standard website.' Butterfield sat down at her desk. 'But it did not really give much detail.'

'There's not much to give and I'm not quite sure how they got the story in the first place,' said the Leicester detective. 'We certainly did not release anything. Not sure it was worth it really – and as far as I know the reporter did not ring up to check his facts. Not exactly professional.'

'The piece was written by a chap called Tony Gerrard, who has just become the editor of our weekly newspaper. Do you know him?'

'No, but they come and go so fast – do reporters on the Standard – that you don't really get the chance. And they never seem to get out of the office. He why you're so interested?'

'Not him but there could be a link to a murder we've had up here. Bloke nailed to a shed last night.'

'Yeah, heard it on the radio news. Exactly how do we come into it?'

'We're trying to work out if Lighting the Way are involved. The newspaper report says they were living at the house in Ravensdale Road.' Butterfield reached out to tap a key on her computer keyboard. 'I'll email you a picture of the victim. It's not a very good scan, I am afraid, a bit dark, but you can just about make him out.'

'Happy to look at it for you, Alison, but I'm not sure I can be much help, and I'd be amazed if Lighting the Way were involved. I didn't have much to do with them but they were quite a peaceable bunch, as I recall. A bit intense but pretty harmless, if you ask me.'

'Yet there was a violent incident at their house?'

'There was, yes, but it was a one-off, and they would appear to have been the innocent victims.'

'What happened?' asked Butterfield. She attached the image of Michael Hills to the email and hit 'send'.

'The trouble was caused by some bloke called…' Butterfield heard a tapping of fingers on a keyboard. 'Ah, yes, here it is, Thomas Oldroyd. Aged 26. Local lad. No record. Well, not since he was a juvenile and even then it was low-level stuff when he was fourteen. Vandalism, scratching cars. Had a couple of spells in psychiatric hospital after he did it. Cops thought that made more sense than charging him.'

'It work?'

'Seems to have. Until Ravensdale Road.'

'What happened?'

'He seems to have turned up at the house in an agitated state. Neighbours called the police when they heard shouting and glass being smashed. It was all over by the time uniform arrived.'

'Has this Oldroyd chap got any connection with Lighting the Way?' asked Butterfield.

'I got the impression that they might have known him, but the only one who answered my questions was some lad called David ... Fulton, I think he was called... and he said they'd never met him. The rest stayed shtum.'

'Sounds familiar. Did they tell you anything useful?'

'From what I could gather, Oldroyd tried to get into the house and one of the Lighting the Way people stopped him. There was a brief scuffle, and Oldroyd punched him in the face then fled, chucking a milk bottle through the front window as he went.'

'You get him?'

'Yeah, uniform picked him up a couple of streets away, but he refused to say why he'd done it. In fact, he hardly spoke at all. The victim did not want to press charges and wasn't really injured, so we let him go.'

'And that's where it ended?'

'Pretty much. We had a load on at the time – it was a weekend and we were short-handed. We'd had two murders so, to be honest, we were not that bothered about a little dust-up like that. I was happy to mark it NFA.'

'Understandable in the circumstances, Stella. You got a name for the bloke he punched, by any chance?'

'Yeah, it's here somewhere.' There was more tapping on the keyboard. 'Radley. Jacob Radley. Aged thirty-five. Lived at the house. We don't know anything else about him. Nothing on file. Not that we did much looking.'

'How come Radley did not want to press charges?'

'If you've met the Lighting the Way people, you know what they're like. They take their religion very seriously. All love and forgiveness. Radley said something about turning the other cheek. If there was anything more to it, no one was telling us. Next time I drove past the house it was empty, so I guess they'd moved on. Did I miss something?'

'Don't think so. It was always a long shot.' Butterfield sighed; she could just imagine the expression on the detective inspector's face when she heard the news. 'My governor said I was wasting my time and it looks like she's right.'

'Exactly what my governor said when the job came in.'

'Thanks for ringing back anyway. You should have that picture now, for what it's worth, although the Internet is pretty slow up here so it could take a while. Depends how fast the mouse is running in its wheel.'

'Got it. I'll just...' Gaunt's voice tailed off.

'You still there?' asked Butterfield.

'Yes, I am.' The Leicester detective's voice was different now. Serious. Troubled. 'This picture. Did you say that it's your murder victim?'

'It is, yes. A bloke called Michael Hills, although we suspect that it's a fake name.'

'I would imagine that it is, Alison. And you can tell your governor that she is wrong, you are not wasting your time. You see, you may know him as Michael Hills but I know him as Jacob Radley. Sounds like you and I have the same victim.'

Butterfield concluded the conversation and looked round the deserted CID room.

'Yes,' she exclaimed in triumph. 'Yes, yes, yes!'

Chapter nine

It was shortly after 9.45am when three vehicles swept out of the yard at Levton Bridge police station and drove at speed along the damp streets, their headlights reflecting off glistening pavements. They emerged onto the valley road and headed in the direction of Bradby village. Harris, who had left Philip Curtis to conduct the press conference, was leading the way in his Land Rover, with a grim-faced Gillian Roberts in the passenger seat, followed by Gallagher and a bright-eyed Butterfield in the sergeant's car and, bringing up the rear, a police van carrying half a dozen officers in riot gear.

Harris leaned forward to see a way through the gloom as the rain drove hard against the vehicle's windscreen while, beside him, Roberts sat in a brooding silence, staring out at the curtain of mist that was obscuring the fields.

'You're very quiet,' said the inspector. He risked a quick glance at his travelling companion as he guided the vehicle round a sharp bend. 'Not like you.'

'I cocked up.' She sighed and looked at him with a disconsolate expression on her face. 'Back there in the briefing, Hawk, I cocked up, and I did it big time in front of everyone else.'

'About the happy clappies?'

'I made a basic error. Thirty years in the force and I allowed myself to make assumptions.' She shook her head then punched the dashboard. 'Stupid, stupid, stupid.'

'If it's any consolation, I did not take them as seriously as I should have either.' Harris manoeuvred the vehicle round another corner. 'It was only when we linked the victim here to the one in Leicester that it started to look iffy.'

'Yes, but it was me pouring all the cold water, wasn't it?' Gloomily, the detective inspector returned her attention to the fields. 'I let myself be shown up by a rookie detective constable who had more gumption than the lot of us put together. If she hadn't chased up Leicester CID, who knows what might have happened?'

'We'd have got there in the end.'

'Maybe we would, but it's not like Butterfield hadn't been trying to warn us, is it?' exclaimed Roberts, her exasperation turning into a flash of anger. 'Jesus, we have enough trouble reigning in the girl's ego as it is. She'll be bloody insufferable after this.'

'She'll learn.'

'And she wasn't the only one trying to warn me. Edie Prentice tried to tell me that there was something off about them but I wouldn't listen.'

'Did she have any evidence?' asked Harris.

'Not as such, just a feeling about David Fulton – said he was rude.'

'Not exactly illegal. Jesus, I'd have been locked up years ago if it was.'

'I know but I just assumed it was old prejudices coming to the surface. I'm not blind to Edie's faults, really I'm not, but I should have listened harder to what she was saying.'

'I wouldn't beat yourself up about it.' Harris wiped a hand across the windscreen to clear away some of the condensation that had built up inside the vehicle. 'It's very rare that you slip up.'

'Thanks for trying to make me feel better, Hawk, but I'd rather wallow in a pathetic slough of self-recrimination, if it's alright with you.'

'Of course. You wallow away.'

Roberts gave a rueful grin, and they both burst into laughter. After a few minutes, though, the detective inspector's mood darkened again as she began to worry about what they would find at the farmhouse. She did not have long to wait as, a few hundred metres before Bradby Village, Harris turned the Land Rover off the road and guided it up a rough, winding track, the vehicle bouncing off the stones as it climbed. Roberts gripped her seat in alarm as they careered round a tight bend and, in the back, the dogs looked anxious as they were thrown about.

'Don't worry about them,' said Harris, noticing Roberts glancing behind her. 'They're used to it.'

'I'm not bothered about the blessed dogs – you're loosening my fillings!'

'Sorry,' said Harris, slowing down slightly. But only slightly.

As the Land Rover pulled into the yard, the detectives saw that the front door of the farmhouse was standing wide open.

'Damn,' said Roberts quietly.

'It would seem that our little friends have scarpered,' said Harris. He got out of the Land Rover and turned up his coat collar against the rain. 'And in my experience, innocent people don't do that.'

The other vehicles arrived, their tyres crunching on the loose stones. Gallagher and Butterfield got out of the sergeant's car and walked over to the Land Rover.

'The minibus has gone,' said Gallagher. He gestured to where the vehicle had been parked the previous evening. 'It would seem that the Good Lord appeared to our friends in a flash of light and told them to have it away on their toes before they got themselves arrested.'

'I feel,' said Roberts before Butterfield could say anything, 'that I owe you an apology, Constable. I should have listened to what you were saying.'

'I'm sure that an apology is not necessary, ma'am,' said Butterfield, trying her best to sound respectful.

'Thank you for your understanding but please allow someone who is old enough to know better to atone for their mistake in whatever grovelling manner she chooses.'

'I'd do as she says,' said Harris. He tapped the side of his nose. 'It's part of the wallowing process.'

'Sir?'

'Never mind.'

A slim young man emerged from the front door of the farmhouse. The inspector eyed his shock of bleached blond hair, sharp grey suit and floral buttonhole without much enthusiasm. The young man, for his part, surveyed the uniformed officers with bemusement as they got out of the van.

'Hello, hello, hello,' he said. 'What's this, I wonder?'

'I wonder,' said the inspector. He walked over and held up his warrant card. 'I'm DCI Harris. And you are?'

'Zak Raynor. No C.'

'And what brings you here this morning, Zak Raynor No C?'

'I might ask you the same thing.'

'You might.'

The silence that followed punctured Raynor's cheeriness and the other officers viewed his mounting discomfort with mild amusement; everyone knew that Jack Harris had little time for young people, especially over-confident ones. Although it had not gone unnoticed among his colleagues that he appeared to make an exception for Alison Butterfield. Even Gillian Roberts felt a bit better at the spectacle of the young man's neck glowing red as he grew increasingly flustered under the inspector's withering stare.

'Well, young man?' said Harris after a few moments. 'Are you going to tell me what you are doing here or do I have to guess?'

'Yes. Yes, of course. I work for Sheldrick and Gunn. We're the letting agents. We've managed the place for Old Man Robinson since he went into the home.'

'And you are here because?'

'We had a message last night from the tenants, saying that they were leaving.'

'But you only bothered to come up this morning?'

'No, it wasn't like that,' said Raynor hurriedly. 'It was left on the answering machine, so it didn't get picked up until the office opened. We only open at nine.'

'Lucky you.'

'The boss sent me straight up. He knows he can trust me, does Mr Sheldrick, and we didn't want the house left unlocked. There was break-in here a couple of nights ago.'

'Is that a fact?'

'Yeah, some bikes got nicked.' Raynor noticed the faintest of smiles on the inspector's face. 'But I imagine you know all that.'

'I imagine I do.' Harris watched the uniformed officers approaching the house and gestured to Gallagher. 'Just you go in to start with, Matty lad. If it *is* a crime scene, I don't want any evidence contaminated. Give it the once over and shout out if you need any help.'

Gallagher waved a hand and disappeared through the front door. The uniformed officers and Butterfield returned to the van to shelter from the rain, leaving Harris and Roberts talking to Zak Raynor.

'Any idea why the tenants went in such a rush?' asked Roberts. 'I take it you didn't know that they were planning to go?'

'No, we didn't and David didn't say why they were leaving in his message.' Raynor's eyes gleamed. 'You said

75

crime scene. Have they done something wrong? Is it something to do with that murder on the radio? I bet it is.'

'And why would you think that, sunbeam?' asked Harris.

'I always thought they were funny sorts, you know.' Raynor lowered his voice. 'A bit shifty. I notice these things. In fact, I always fancied being a detective.'

'And yet you ended up as a gopher,' said Harris.

Raynor looked offended.

'Assistant Administration Executive,' he said.

'My apologies,' said Harris. 'Assistant Gopher. Well shifty or not, we are keen to talk to them.'

'In which case,' said Raynor, desperate to gain face after the inspector's comment, 'I might have some information that will interest you.'

He paused for effect.

'Well, what is it?' snapped Harris, glaring at him. 'I am not in the mood to play games, son.'

'Sorry, yes, well, they are behind on their rent. Six weeks.'

'So much for the Good Lord paying the bills,' murmured Harris, thinking back to his conversation with the vicar the previous evening. 'However, I suspect that this may be about more than a few weeks' unpaid rent.'

'Do you know where they have gone, by any chance?' asked Roberts. 'David Fulton leave a forwarding address?'

'I am afraid not. It's all a bit sudden.'

'It certainly is,' said Harris. He watched as Gallagher re-emerged from the house. 'Well?'

'Yeah, they've definitely gone,' said the sergeant. 'No clothes in the wardrobes, no bags. Door key left on the kitchen table.'

Gillian Roberts closed her eyes.

'No note?' asked Harris.

'Zilch. Looks like they just upped and went. Not long after we left them last night, I am guessing. We must have spooked them.' He looked at Raynor. 'What time was the message left on your answering machine?'

'Eleven thirty, I think.'

'Yeah, just after we left.' Gallagher frowned. 'I should have listened to Alison. She said we should go back in.'

'God, not two of us apologising to her!' exclaimed Roberts. 'She'll be wanting to be chief constable next!'

Harris said nothing but stared across the hills for a few moments. As ever at times like this, the inspector wished that he was up on the tops where the buzzards roamed free, him and his dogs, loping long and easy over the moors. The ringing of Gallagher's mobile phone disturbed his reverie and Harris watched as the sergeant took the call and walked across the yard, deep in conversation, occasionally pacing in circles as he talked and became increasingly animated.

Zak Raynor's mobile phone also rang.

'My office,' he explained, taking the device out of his jacket pocket and reading the caller ID. 'What do I tell them?'

'I'm sure you'll think of something,' said Harris. 'A high-flying corporate executive of your calibre.'

'So, what do you reckon, Hawk?' asked Roberts as Raynor took the call and moved out of earshot. She looked at the house. 'Have we just let our prime suspects slip through our fingers?'

'Do you know, Gillian, I'm not sure that we have.'

'You're not?' The relief was clear in her voice. 'Hang on, though; you said yourself that fleeing like this is suspicious behaviour.'

'But it could also be the actions of frightened people, could it not? What if they are victims?'

'Victims?' said the detective inspector.

'What if Matty and Alison put the fear of God into them last night? What if they thought they were here because there was a link with the murder? Maybe they feared that this Oldroyd lad might be involved? That he

77

had come after them again? Maybe they took fright and headed off into the night?'

'But why not tell us? Let us protect them?'

'Would you? Levton Bridge has hardly welcomed them, has it? Maybe it was easier to run away.'

'Actually, that makes sense,' said Roberts.

'Don't sound so surprised.'

'Sorry.' She sounded more cheerful now. 'Yes, I'll buy that. It fits in much better with what we know of them. And this Oldroyd guy does sound like he's a bit of a crackerjack.'

'Certainly crackerjack enough to put the wind up a bunch of peace-loving innocents.'

'And what about him?' asked Roberts. She nodded towards Zak Raynor, who was now walking in circles on the far side of the yard, deep in animated conversation with his office. 'What do we make of Barry Chuckle?'

'Who?'

'You can tell you never had children. I mean young Zak. With no C. Is he tied up in this?'

'No, I reckon he's alright.'

'But he *was* here when we arrived.'

Harris frowned. 'Maybe worth putting a call in to his office just to make sure, then,' he said. 'You're right about us assuming too many things.'

'I'll give Stan Sheldrick a ring. He'll give me the low-down.' Roberts watched Gallagher end his call and stride purposefully towards them. 'Now there's a man with news to impart.'

'That was a pal of mine at forensics,' said the sergeant. There was a gleam in his eyes as he walked up to them. 'She's been doing a bit of digging, and you're going to love what she's come up with. Absolutely love it.'

'I wouldn't bet on it,' grunted Harris. 'What did she say?'

'The fingerprints of the man we know as Michael Hills match those from a bloke who was arrested for punching a fellow in Leicester.'

'Another Leicester link,' said Harris.

'Indeed so,' said Gallagher. 'What's more, the incident happened in a pub not far from the house in Ravensdale Road where Thomas Oldroyd got into a fracas with Lighting the Way. Same weekend, in fact. The fingerprints were taken when uniform arrested the man we know as Michael Hills for assault.'

'Which means we can definitely put a name to him,' said Harris. 'I am assuming it is this Jacob Radley fellow that Stella Gaunt mentioned?'

'Ah, would it were that simple,' said Gallagher. He was enjoying himself. 'You see, the man we think is Michael Hills and who Leicester CID reckon is Jacob Radley gave the name John Halstead when he was arrested after the incident in the pub, which explains why Stella did not make the connection.

'Looks like we've got a right little conman on our hands,' said Roberts. 'Multiple identities, it's classic behaviour. But, like Hawk says, at least we've got a name for him now.'

'A name, yes, just not *his* name.' Gallagher paused for effect. 'See, when John Halstead was murdered on the allotment last night, he'd already been dead for six months!'

Harris and Roberts stared at him in astonishment. Gallagher beamed, revelling in the impact that his words were having.

'What do you mean dead?' said Harris.

'Brown bread.'

'Yes, that's enough of your quaint Cockney terminology,' grunted Harris. 'Let's have it in English.'

'It seems that John Halstead died in an RTA two days after being bailed for the punch-up in the boozer. Good, eh?'

'Are you sure about this?' asked Roberts. 'Forensics not stringing you a line? Some of them have a very strange sense of humour, you know.'

'No, it's straight up. A bloke answering to the name of John Halstead was driving a Nissan Micra that crashed on the M1 late at night, not far from Leicester. The vehicle came off the road for no reason, hit a bridge and burst into flames. Police found a badly burned body and the charred remains of a driving licence which suggested it was him. Plus, the car was a hire vehicle that had been taken out in his name the day before.'

'But did not the fingerprints suggest it was someone else?' asked Harris.

'No prints. His hands were too badly damaged. You can't really blame the traffic cops for deciding it was him, mind. As far as they were concerned, they had a straightforward RTA on their hands. Except clearly it wasn't.'

'Very little is straightforward about our Mr Hills,' said Harris. 'The question is why would he go to such remarkable lengths to hide his true identity? What was he trying to hide?'

'Or hide from. Thomas Oldroyd assaulted him at the house in Leicester, remember. What odds that Oldroyd was the man he assaulted in the pub the next night?' Gallagher gestured to the house. 'Maybe Hills or whatever he's called was trying to keep out of his way as well, just like this lot.

'Maybe,' said Harris. 'One thing is certain; we won't be able to relax until we've tracked Oldroyd down. I want him arrested and arrested quickly. The last thing I want is him running round our patch scaring the bejasus out of people. Do we know anything about him?'

'Not really,' said Gallagher. 'I got the office to double-check criminal records before we came out but, like Stella Gaunt says, there's nothing on file apart from a few incidents when he was a nipper. And there's no soft intelligence about him either. Rather like our dead man, Thomas Oldroyd is a bit of a mystery.'

'And I don't like mysteries,' said Harris.

* * *

The police patrol vehicle pulled into the lay-by shortly after 10am and the two uniformed officers sat for a few moments and surveyed the silver BMW parked in front of them.

'That's it alright,' said the officer in the passenger seat. He glanced down at a piece of paper lying on his lap. 'According to the woman who rang it in, she saw it parked here late last night, and it was still here when she came past this morning on her way to work. She thought it looked a bit suspicious.'

'And it's definitely the one that Levton Bridge CID are looking for?' said the driver.

'Yeah, belongs to some bloke called McGuffin who went missing last night. CID reckon that it might be connected to that murder on the allotment.'

'Nasty business,' said the driver. 'We'd best take a look-see.'

He got out of the vehicle, turned his collar up against the driving rain and walked over to the BMW. The officer leaned over to peer into the driver's window but, on seeing no one there, looked through the rear side window. He shook his head as his colleague joined him.

'Nothing,' he said.

'We'd best search the copse just to be sure,' said his colleague, joining him.

The officers entered the shadows of the trees, the fresh smell of dripping pine leaves hanging heavy and pungent in the air and their feet squelching on the spongy carpet of damp moss. They had almost reached the end of the trees and could see the cows grazing peacefully in the field that lay beyond, when both officers stopped.

'Shit,' murmured the driver.

They stood for a few moments and stared in silent horror at the man who had been nailed to a tree, his hands twisted above his head, and his skull split open by a vicious blow that had exposed part of his brain and created crimson rivers that streamed down his face. The driver edged his way forwards and felt his stomach twist and knot as he stared into the dead, dark eyes of Dennis McGuffin.

Chapter ten

'Well?' said Harris as Gallagher clumped down the farmhouse stairs and emerged into the yard amid rain that had now slowed to a light drizzle. 'Have forensics come up with anything?

'Nothing,' said the sergeant. 'They're going to do a more detailed search, but there's no sign of disturbance. If John Halstead was taken from here last night, he went peaceably.'

Harris pointed to a man in a set of white overalls who was crouched down a few metres away,

'Bob reckons there's a set of tyre tracks that suggest that another vehicle was here,' he said.

'Maybe it *was* Thomas Oldroyd then,' said Roberts. 'Come to finish what he started, like you said.'

'Maybe it was,' said Harris. 'All roads seem to be leading to him at the moment.'

Butterfield walked over to the officers and held up her mobile phone.

'It's Stella Gaunt at Leicester CID,' she said. The constable pressed a button on the device. 'I've put her on speaker.'

'Hi, everyone,' said the Leicester detective.

'Hello, Stella, this is DCI Jack Harris,' said the inspector.

'The bird man, if I am not mistaken.'

'How do you know that?' asked Harris, whose other role with the force was as a part-time wildlife liaison officer.

'I used to work a rural patch in Rutland and they sent me to a lecture you gave on poisoning. It was at a hotel near Coventry. I talked to you afterwards. Don't suppose you remember me but it was very useful. We nicked a guy for killing red kite because of what you said that day.'

'Good for you,' said Harris; anyone who showed an interest in wildlife immediately went up in the inspector's estimation.

He tried to remember their conversation but could not bring her to mind. The inspector resisted the temptation to ask what she looked like; he knew what the others would be thinking. He was aware of the rumours about his private life but did little to dampen them down.

'So, what did you find out about the incident in the pub?' asked Harris instead. 'Was our dead guy there?'

'He was indeed but not under the name Michael Hills. He told our officers he was called John Halstead, which is why no one connected the incidents. Unfortunately, the bloke he punched ran off after it happened, but uniform got a description. Long black hair, long black coat and shiny black boots – and that's how Thomas Oldroyd usually dresses. He cuts a very striking figure, apparently. Bit of a Goth.'

'Any idea why it happened?' asked the inspector.

'Halstead seems to have been drinking with four other people – I am guessing it was David Fulton and his friends – and Oldroyd came into the pub and started an argument with them.'

'What about?' asked Harris. The inspector nodded at Gillian Roberts as she took a call on her mobile, waved a hand to excuse herself from the conservation and walked across to the other side of the yard. 'What were they arguing about?'

'Uniform didn't seem sure,' said Stella. 'But whatever it was, it infuriated Halstead so much that he hit Oldroyd.'

'Not very peaceable,' said Harris.

'I guess even peaceable people have their limits.'

Harris recalled a similar comment made by the vicar during their conversation the previous evening.

'I guess they do,' he said. 'It must have been something pretty serious for Halstead to abandon his principles, though. I mean, when Oldroyd went for him the night before he didn't even want to press charges.'

'Uniform didn't really get into the whys and wherefores, I am afraid. It was a busy Saturday night so they bailed Halstead after a couple of hours because they needed the cell.'

'DS Gallagher here,' said the sergeant, walking over to be nearer the phone. 'What do you know about the car crash? Clearly, it wasn't John Halstead in the vehicle.'

'I checked it out with Traffic. Everything pointed to it being him at the time but they couldn't find any relatives, so they had to go on what they had. It all checked out, mind, including his address.'

'Ravensdale Road?' asked the sergeant.

'No, he was renting a city centre flat.'

'Any idea who the body in the car really was then?' asked Harris. He tried to concentrate on the conversation but was becoming increasingly distracted by the grim expression on Gillian Roberts' face as she spoke on her mobile.

'We're checking our missing persons list. We know that it was a man, but we can't do DNA because he was cremated.'

'Again,' said Gallagher. He allowed himself a smile at his joke and an even broader one when he saw Harris's pained expression.

'He your office comedian?' said Stella.

'Something like that,' grunted Harris as Gallagher grinned.

'We all have them,' said Stella Gaunt. 'Listen, my governor thinks that I should come up since it looks like we're going to be working the same case. Would that be OK, sir?'

'Good idea,' said Harris; he'd finally remembered what she looked like. A willowy blonde if he recalled correctly. Harris liked willowy blondes. 'Sort it out with Alison. I look forward to seeing you again.'

'Same here.'

Gallagher gave his boss a sly look as Butterfield walked away, deep in conversation with Stella on the mobile.

'You're a dirty dog,' said the sergeant, when he was sure that the constable was out of earshot.

'My interest in DC Gaunt is entirely professional, Matty lad.'

'Yeah, I'll bet it is.' Matty Gallagher. 'She a looker then?'

'Her appearance is of little interest to me,' replied Harris. 'Indeed, I can't even remember meeting the girl.'

Gallagher decided that the slight twitch of the inspector's lips betrayed the detective's true feelings.

'Of course, you can't,' said the sergeant.

'So, what we got?' said Harris, secretly enjoying the exchange. 'Thomas Oldroyd gets hacked off at the way Halstead stands up to him at the house, fancies seconds and tracks him down to the pub for another go the following evening?'

'Something like that,' said Gallagher. He smiled inwardly at the way the inspector had changed the subject. 'There was clearly plenty of bad feeling between the two of them.'

'Then what? Halstead smacks Oldroyd and the Lighting the Way folks get frightened that he might take revenge and come here only for Oldroyd to track them down?'

'Could be.'

'Good enough for a working theory, at any rate,' said Harris as Roberts finished her phone call and walked over to them. 'Looks like your instincts were right all along, Gillian. There's no way that this lot carried out our murder.'

'Not *this* murder, maybe.' Her voice was low and solemn.

'What do you mean?'

'A couple of traffic officers have just found a man nailed to a tree in a wood near the turn off for the M6. They reckon it could be Dennis McGuffin. His car's parked in the lay-by.' The detective inspector sighed. 'And who were the last people to have a dust up with him?'

'Did you get a description out on the minibus?' asked Harris, looking at Gallagher.

'Sure did.'

'Well, get it sent out again, will you? Make it top priority. Oh, and get one out on Thomas Oldroyd as well. I want him arrested and I want it done fast.'

The detectives turned as a car drove into the yard and came to a halt. They watched as the driver turned in his seat and, for a moment, it looked as if he was about to reverse and make his escape. When a couple of uniformed officers moved into position to block his way, he thought better of the idea and turned to face forwards again. Harris gestured for him to get out of the vehicle, which he did to reveal himself as a young man with tousled jet-black hair and wearing a long black leather coat and shiny black boots. As he walked over to the officers, the coat flapped open to reveal a black T-shirt emblazoned with the words Jesus Is Watching You.

'I fancy I know who you are,' said Harris.

'My name is Thomas Oldroyd,' said the young man calmly. 'And since you're here, I wish to make a confession.'

'I'll bet you do, sunshine.'

'I know you said fast,' said Roberts. She shook her head as she watched the inspector slip the handcuffs on Oldroyd's wrists. 'But this is remarkable, even by your standards.'

'When you've got it, you've got it,' said Harris.

Chapter eleven

'Are you sure that this is all really necessary?' said Henry Grace as he held his front door open to allow James Larch and two uniformed officers to enter the narrow hallway of his house. 'I told you last night that it was only a few words with the man.'

'I am afraid that Dennis McGuffin has been murdered,' said Larch. 'His body was found this morning, and we need you to come down to the station to answer a few questions.'

'Dear God,' said Grace. He leaned weakly against the wall and looked at the detective constable in horror. 'Hang on; surely you do not think that I could possibly be the one who…?'

'You might need a solicitor,' said Larch.

'This is ridiculous!' protested Grace. 'I am a respectable man, and there is no way that I could ever do something like that! Why on earth would you think any different?'

'We need to talk to anyone who might have wished Mr McGuffin harm.'

'Harm!' exclaimed Grace. He started to struggle as he was led down the hall by one of the uniformed officers.

'For God's sake man, Dennis may have been irritating, but there's no way I would ever wish him harm. It was only an argument about a letter. I shall be making an official complaint to your superior officer.'

'I am sure that DCI Harris will be happy to consider it,' said Larch, ignoring the protestations. 'Are you going to come with us peaceably?'

'No, I am not!' Grace continued to struggle. 'In fact, as far as I am concerned, this is a flagrant infringement of...'

'You have a choice, Mr Grace,' said the other uniformed officer. 'You can come with us voluntarily, or DC Larch here can arrest you, and we'll march you out to our car in handcuffs.'

'And what would people think if they saw that happen?' asked Larch. 'Not sure it would do much for your reputation within the community, would it now? Your choice, Mr Grace.'

Henry Grace sighed.

'Just let me get my coat,' he said. 'But you're making a terrible mistake.'

As Henry Grace was led into the street a few moments later, Edie Prentice turned the corner and saw him being helped into the back seat of the police vehicle. She gave a cry and hurried up to the officers.

'Let him go!' she exclaimed, grabbing one of the uniformed officer's arms as he tried to close the door.

'What do you think you are doing?' said the officer, shrugging her off.

'Henry has done nothing wrong!' Edie glared at James Larch. 'I shall be making a formal complaint, of that you can be sure!'

'Might I suggest,' said Larch as he swung himself into the front passenger street, 'that you get in the queue.'

* * *

Jack Harris stood at the top of the police station steps and surveyed the massed ranks of journalists staring expectantly up at him. A battery of television cameras was trained on the inspector, and several reporters held out tape recorders; he could hear the whirring of the devices. There was a sense of excitement as the journalists waited for the inspector to provide new revelations.

'What can you tell us, Chief Inspector?' shouted one of the reporters.

'In addition to what Superintendent Curtis told you earlier this morning, I can now confirm that a second person has been found murdered,' said Harris.

A buzz ran round the assembled gathering.

'The body was found near Hawsham this morning,' continued Harris. 'We are not releasing the name of either victim just yet, and it is far too early to provide much more information.'

'Is either of the victims the Chairman of the Parochial Church Council?' shouted a reporter. 'A man called Dennis McGuffin, who went missing last night? Is there any truth in that?'

'Like I said, we will release their identities in due course.'

'Any truth in the rumour that the victim last night was crucified?' shouted another reporter. 'Is this a religiously-motivated hate crime, Chief Inspector?'

Harris hesitated; everyone knew that the rules changed when an offence was labelled a hate crime. People who normally took no notice suddenly started getting involved when something was attributed to religious hatred. Antennae started twitching in the Home Office, and senior officers at headquarters started to look anxious.

'I am not going to release information about cause of death,' said the inspector eventually. 'Or speculate on motives.'

'Any truth in suggestions that you are investigating a religious group called Lighting the Way in connection with what has happened?' asked another reporter.

'A number of people have been assisting us in our enquiries. I am not prepared to comment on their identities.'

'Come on, Chief Inspector, give us something.'

Noticing the patrol car containing Henry Grace turn into the street from the marketplace and head down the hill towards the police station, Harris decided that he needed to distract the media's attention before they worked out what was happening. The last thing he wanted was the journalists hearing that the President of the Rotary Club had been arrested. Hate crime was one thing, but bitter experience had taught him that arresting someone from the Rotary Club was guaranteed to exercise minds in headquarters even more.

'What I can say,' he continued, 'is that these are vicious crimes and myself and my team are determined to bring the perpetrators to book as soon as possible. We would appeal to the community to stay calm, though. We have already had a number of calls to the control room from concerned members of the public, but everything we have discovered so far leads us to believe that these are targeted crimes and that the wider community is not at risk.'

'But you are not prepared to tell us what leads you to that conclusion?'

'No.' Harris saw the patrol car slip unnoticed into the station yard, gave a sigh of relief and turned on his heel. 'And I am not prepared to be drawn into further speculation either. The Press Office will keep you informed.'

'Yes, but isn't it your responsibility to tell us what's happening?' asked a radio journalist as the detective pushed open the front door. 'You are the senior officer, after all.'

Harris turned back to face them.

'My responsibility,' he said, 'is to find out who committed these crimes. Yours, might I suggest, ladies and gentlemen, is not to peddle half-truths.'

'Even if they *are* truths, Chief Inspector?'

Harris stalked back into the police station's reception area. Once away from the clamour of protests from the journalists, he was about to go through the security door into the back office when a woman scurried in through the front door and called his name. The inspector turned to see an elderly woman in a pale blue cardigan and a tweed jacket.

'Detective Inspector Prentice,' he said bleakly. 'I wondered when you'd turn up.'

'What did you call me?'

'Nothing.' He tried to look accommodating. 'How can I assist you, as if I didn't know?'

'Why have you arrested Henry Grace?' demanded Edie. 'He's not done anything wrong.'

'I am not at liberty to…'

'Is it true that Dennis's body has been found?'

'I don't know where you heard…'

'One of the journalists told me.'

'Did they now?'

Harris turned to push his way through the door, but she grabbed his arm, quickly removing it when he glared at her.

'I'm sorry,' she said. The bluster had been replaced by something more vulnerable. 'I'm just worried. Everyone is. I mean, what if one of us is next? People are scared.'

'Look,' said the inspector, softening his tone. 'I know that you are concerned about what has happened, but I really can't comment further until…'

'Dennis was only doing what he had to,' said Edie Prentice. The anger was back. 'We all supported him one hundred per cent. We had to kick those horrible young people out of St Cuthbert's. Coming here with their outlandish ideas.'

'Outlandish ideas? Surely all they want to do is praise God like you do?'

'Yes, but there are ways to do it, Chief Inspector.'

'In what way was their approach wrong, Edie?'

'They were too,' she hesitated as she searched for the word. 'Fervent. Yes, that's it. Fervent. All that shouting out and waving their hands in services. It's very off-putting, you know. We had all on to stop them doing it.'

'Why stop them, Edie? You're all the same, I would have thought.'

'You sound just like *them*,' she said.

And Edie Prentice turned and walked out of the station.

'Which,' murmured Harris as he walked out behind her and watched her stride along the street, waving aside questions from the waiting journalists, 'would appear to be a crime in this town.'

Harris was just about to turn back into the station when he saw another familiar figure walking purposefully towards him.

'God give me strength,' he said with a sigh.

He hurried back into the reception area and was about to go through the door into the corridor when he heard the voice.

'Chief Inspector!' shouted Harry Osborne. 'Not trying to avoid me, I hope?'

'Of course not,' said Harris through gritted teeth. He turned to face the allotment committee chairman. 'Always a pleasure. And what can I do for you?'

'I demand an explanation!' said Osborne angrily. 'Your officers are preventing the plot holders from getting to their allotments.'

'That's right. Forensics have not completed their examination of the site yet.'

'Yes, well, I just hope they're not trampling all over the vegetables.'

'I'm sure…'

'What's more, I understand that you are interviewing my members. I've had a number of calls. They are very upset about the insinuations that your officers are making. And is it true that you have arrested Henry Grace?'

'It's purely…'

'You've lost the plot, man! Whatever is behind this awful business, it's nothing to do with the allotments.'

'Then why is Dennis McGuffin dead?'

Osborne stared at the inspector in disbelief. Shock replaced anger.

'Dennis dead?' he said in a hollow voice. 'Are you sure?

'I am,' said Harris. He pushed his way through the door. 'So, you'll forgive me if I don't worry about your vegetables.'

Chapter twelve

'So,' said Jack Harris, staring across the interview room desk at the impassive Thomas Oldroyd, who was sitting with his arms folded and calmly returning the detective's gaze, 'you want to confess then?'

Oldroyd nodded but said nothing. It had been like that for the past hour and a half and Harris watched the young man with growing bemusement. Not normally someone who found himself drawn to people – Jack Harris was an animal person – the inspector nevertheless found himself fascinated by the suspect. Oldroyd's calm demeanour had remained unruffled, and he had not spoken when Harris cautioned him for the murders when he was arrested in the farmyard.

On the journey to Levton Bridge Police Station in the police van, Oldroyd ignored officers' attempts to talk to him and instead stared out at the expanses of water beginning to pool on the windswept fields. His silence had continued when he got to the police station where he had been bundled into the building, his head covered in a blanket to avoid the press photographers' lenses as the van pushed its way past the throng of excited journalists.

Once inside, Oldroyd had seemed impervious to the looks from officers and civilians alike as they stared in fascination at a man who was capable of crucifying his victims. His only response had been the slightest of smiles at one point, as if he knew something they did not. Watching him now in the stuffy little windowless room with the bare white walls, Harris cast around for the best word to describe his demeanour. Serenity, that was the word, he decided eventually; Thomas Oldroyd was exuding serenity as if the world was passing him by. As if the seriousness of the situation held little anxiety for him.

Not for the first time in the past fourteen hours, Jack Harris thought about faith and fancied that he sensed greater powers than he at work. The inspector shook his head to banish the fanciful thought, replacing it with concern that, despite his composed demeanour, Thomas Oldroyd maybe really did not understand what was happening.

'So, what do you want to confess to?' asked Harris.

'Not the murders of those men you mentioned,' replied Oldroyd; his voice was quiet but confident. 'I have never heard of that McGuffin bloke and I might not like Michael Hills, as he pretended he was called, but I would never kill him.'

'So, what name did you know him by?'

'John Halstead. His little charade did not fool me. I'm not saying that Halstead did not deserve to be murdered for his betrayal of those who took him into their hearts, Chief Inspector, but I would never resort to something like that. To commit murder goes against all my beliefs.'

'Not to mention the law of the land.'

'*Your* land, Chief Inspector.'

'I like to think so,' said Harris. 'Anyway, whatever he's called, you do admit to knowing him?'

'I do not think that knowing someone is a crime to which one should admit, Chief Inspector. We are all brothers in the eyes of the Lord, are we not? Even sinners like John Halstead.'

'I'm sure we are.' Harris sighed; he was already starting to grow weary of Oldroyd's sanctimonious attitude. The inspector decided that he preferred the silent version. 'Look, are you sure you don't want a solicitor? This is a serious matter, and I am not quite sure that you realise the extent...'

'I do not require a solicitor, no, and I am entirely aware of what you are trying to do, but we will all be judged on the day of reckoning.'

'Yes, well, if you feel the need for someone more temporal, do let me know,' replied Harris. 'Although I do know the odd solicitor who thinks he's God.'

Oldroyd allowed himself a smile at the comment.

'I will do,' he said. 'Thank you.'

It seemed to the inspector that, for the first time since he had been arrested, Thomas Oldroyd had come over as human, the first time he had offered a glimpse of himself. The thought encouraged the detective.

'So, if you don't want to admit to the murders,' said Harris, 'what do you want to confess to?'

'That I assaulted John Halstead in Leicester six months ago. At the house in Ravensdale Avenue.'

'Is that all?' Harris could not hide his disappointment.

'It may not be much to you, Chief Inspector, but it has weighed heavily on my conscience ever since it happened.' Oldroyd's face assumed a troubled expression. 'I am a peaceable man, and I should not have done it. I have spent the past six months seeking absolution for my sin.'

'Well, Ravensdale Road is as good a place to begin with as any, I suppose. An officer from Leicester is coming up here so she can take this forward when she arrives but why not tell me why you attacked him anyway? And why were you trying to force your way into the house? What have you got against Lighting the Way?'

'I will only tell a priest.'

'What?'

'I will only confess my sin to a priest,' repeated Oldroyd. 'You are not a priest.'

'It doesn't work that way, sunbeam,' said Harris. He leaned forward to give him one of his hard stares. 'I'm the power and the glory in this town, and you would do well to remember it so either you tell me what happened or you tell no one.'

'Then I tell no one.' Oldroyd placed his hands on the table. 'You have nothing to prove that I carried out those murders, nor will you find anything. And you only have my word for it that I assaulted John Halstead. All I have to do is sit here and wait for your time to run out; then you will have to release me, and your colleague from Leicester will have had a wasted journey.'

'For a man with no criminal record, you seem to know your way around the criminal justice system.'

'My father is a barrister.' Oldroyd gave another of his knowing smiles. 'Not that he has spoken to me for ten years. He disapproves of my lifestyle. It does not fit in with his worldview. He takes a somewhat more conventional view of things.'

'I imagine he does. You do not want me to call him then? I really do think that you could do with some legal representation.'

'I do not think that would be a good idea, Chief Inspector. Besides, I'm not sure that my father would be minded to help. So, what's it to be – are you going to call a priest or are we going to sit here in companionable silence?'

Harris looked at him for a few moments, not quite sure what to make of such an act of cool defiance. The chief inspector was not accustomed to suspects ignoring his stare, but he knew that Oldroyd was right; he had nothing to link Oldroyd with the killings and a minor assault in Leicester was scant grounds to keep him in custody.

'So, if I do bring a priest in,' said Harris eventually, 'and I'm not saying that I will, you will definitely talk to him? Tell him what happened?'

'It depends.'

'On what?'

'Who it is.'

'You do know that the presence of a clergyman will not save you, I take it?' said Harris. 'We will be at liberty to use anything you say to him in interview as evidence should the case go to court.'

'So be it,' said Oldroyd. 'Can I ask who the priest will be? Not Jim Miles, by any chance?'

'You know him?' asked Harris in surprise.

'I do, yes.'

'How come you….?'

'I am sure that Jim will be only too happy to tell you that,' said Oldroyd. 'Well, I say happy…'

And after another smile that suggested that behind his calm demeanour lurked a sense of humour, Thomas Oldroyd closed his eyes and spoke no more. A man, Harris could not help thinking, at peace with his world. Wherever it may be.

Harris stood up and left the interview room to see Philip Curtis striding down the corridor.

'The media have arrived at Bradby,' said the commander. 'Uniform had to threaten a couple of them with arrest because they were trying to take photographs of the house. I'm worried that this may spiral out of control, Jack.'

'You and me both.'

The two men started to walk down the corridor in the direction of the stairs.

'I am particularly worried that some people are describing this as a religiously-motivated hate crime,' said Curtis. 'You know what that means. People who have no business sticking their neb in, getting involved. They're already twitchy at headquarters, and it won't be long before some chinless wonder from the Home Office rings up. Religion changes everything.'

'Think how much better the world would be without love and peace.'

Curtis gave a slight smile.

'You've been in the job too long,' he said.

'So people tell me.' They started walking up the stairs.

'Talking of love and peace,' said Curtis, 'I have had a woman on called Edie Prentice who seems to possess little of either. Why *exactly* have you arrested Henry Grace?'

'He had a bust up with Dennis McGuffin.'

'From what I hear, so did half the town. Surely it's not enough evidence to pull in such a prominent local citizen?' said Curtis as they reached the top of the stairs. 'Are you sure that young Larch handled things correctly?'

'It's possible that he went a touch over the top,' said Harris as they paused outside his office. 'All I did was ask him to bring him in to give a statement. Larch seems to have arrested him when he resisted.'

'Well, when he's given his statement, get him out of here as quick as you can. I've already had the Chief on demanding to know what's happening. They play golf together, you know.'

Chapter thirteen

Matty Gallagher saw the patrol cars parked in the lay-by and drew his vehicle to a halt on the side of the road. He and Gillian Roberts got out and splashed their way towards the uniformed officer standing at the entrance, the water dripping from his cap as the rain drove down ever harder. After a brief conversation with him, the detectives ducked under the tape that sealed off the site and walked over to the forensics officers who were examining Dennis McGuffin's BMW.

'Anything, Mike?' asked Gallagher to the backside of an officer who was leaning into the back seat of the BMW.

The officer's head emerged.

'Nothing yet, Sarge.' He gestured towards the copse, which was growing increasingly dark. 'Chummy's in there. Right at the far side. Hope you didn't have a big breakfast. He's not a pretty sight.'

'Same as the other one?' asked Gallagher.

'Yeah, pretty much. A real mess. Whoever did this is fucked up in the head, if you ask me.'

The detectives did not speak as they entered the damp peace of the woodland. Too peaceful, thought Gallagher as they walked deeper into the shadows, the noise of their feet muffled by the spongy carpet; no sound, no birds singing, the trees still and silent, nothing moving in the oppressive atmosphere. A man who had spent his first thirty-two years in London, surrounded by noise and clamour, he had always struggled with the North Pennines. Too quiet. Too far from London.

Struck by how divorced from the rest of the world he felt in the wood, the sergeant shivered and glanced nervously around him.

'You feel it too, then,' said Roberts.

'It's certainly oppressive.'

'City boy,' she said affectionately.

'Oddly enough, they also had trees in Bermondsey. And I even saw a flower one day. There was panic in the streets. At least one old dear threw herself under a bus to get away from it.'

Roberts chuckled, the sergeant grinned, and the detectives walked for a few more moments, glad of the light relief.

'You didn't see the body last night, did you?' said Gallagher eventually.

'Seen the pictures, which was enough. Not sure anyone deserves that, whatever they have done.'

'It's funny, when we were standing in the allotment on a nice sunny evening, I didn't feel nervous but here…' The sergeant peered into the shadows again. 'Mike's right, we're dealing with some sick minds here.'

'Do you reckon that our Mister Oldroyd might be one of them?'

'Difficult to tell.' Gallagher frowned. 'It is hard to equate the man we saw back there with this level of violence. I watched him when Harris did the arrest, and either Oldroyd didn't realise what was happening or he genuinely was not concerned. I'm not sure how to describe it really.'

'He's got inner peace has our Mister Oldroyd.'

'I am afraid I don't believe in all that guff,' said the sergeant.

'Well, I do, Matty. I think Oldroyd's calm comes from a sincerely-held faith.'

Gallagher stopped walking and looked at her in surprise.

'That's all a bit deep,' he said. 'You religious then?'

'I used to be,' said Roberts. 'Went to church every Sunday.'

'Didn't have you down for a God-botherer.'

'Well, I was. My parents were both big churchgoers and took us every week as kids. My father was a very devout man. In fact, when I was a teenager, there was a time when I thought I'd like to be a vicar.'

'It was serious then,' said Gallagher as they started walking again. 'Why didn't you go for it?'

'In those days, the Anglican Church would not have anything to do with women priests so I decided to be a copper instead. Then I got married and the boys came along, and I fell out of the habit.'

'As it were.'

'Indeed,' she said with a smile. 'You ever go to church, Matty?'

'Na, not me,' said Gallagher with a laugh as they skirted a large moss-covered tree trunk that was blocking the path. 'The folks tried to get me into it when I was a kid – I was a bit of a scallywag and they thought it might straighten me out – but they gave up in the end. I think they could see they were wasting their time.'

'I hadn't really thought about it in a long time but, for some reason, it all came back to me when I heard about Lighting the Way from Edie a couple of weeks ago. I even started considering going to church again.'

'Why? St Cuthbert's is hardly what you expect from a church, surely. Not with Dennis McGuffin in charge anyway.'

This time, it was the detective inspector who stopped walking.

'I know that,' she said. 'Edie and most of the other parishioners detested Lighting the Way. All that evangelical stuff was anathema to them, but to me it sounded more honest.'

'Not sure it does anything for me,' said Gallagher as they resumed their walking through the wood.

'It's not for everyone, I know that,' said Roberts. 'But something about their approach appealed to me. Trouble is, it made me dismiss what you and Alison Butterfield were saying. I got so angry at the bigotry shown by people like McGuffin and Edie that I did not want to believe what I was hearing.'

'Easy mistake to make.'

'It's kind of you to say so, Matty, but you know as well as I do that a police officer cannot afford to lose their objectivity... oh, my.'

The officers had rounded a tree and stopped to stare at the forensics officer busying himself around the crucified body.

'I never thought I'd see the like,' said the detective inspector in a quiet voice as her gaze took in the scene.

She gulped a couple of times to dampen down the bile that was rising sharp and acrid in her throat.

'You alright?' asked Gallagher.

She nodded.

'I will be,' she said. 'In a minute or two. Just a bit of a shock.'

The detectives walked up to the forensics officer, who turned as they approached.

'Whatcha got?' asked Gallagher.

'Same MO as the one last night,' he said.

Roberts stared in silence at the nails that had been driven into the hands, tearing flesh and splintering bone, and at the bloodied gash in the forehead. She turned her attention to the twisted look on Dennis McGuffin's face, a look that came from deep within eyes that were wide with terror.

'What was that you were saying about inner peace?' said Gallagher.

* * *

'Where is Detective Chief Inspector Harris?' asked Henry Grace. 'I will only talk to someone senior.'

He sat back at the desk in the interview room at Levton Bridge Police Station, folded his arms and stared defiantly at James Larch and his young colleague, Detective Constable Alistair Marshall.

Grace's lawyer, a slim dark-suited man, nodded his agreement.

'It certainly seems odd that something this serious should be handled by two officers of such junior rank,' he said.

'DCI Harris is engaged on other enquiries,' said Larch.

'Does he even know that you have arrested me?' asked Grace.

'Yes, of course he does. It was the DCI who suggested we bring you in to give a statement.'

'I can't help feeling you've gone beyond that, Constable,' said the solicitor.

'Jack Harris needs his head examining,' said Grace. 'What's more, he clearly does not regard me as a genuine suspect if he can't be bothered to come and interview me himself.'

'DCI Harris is perfectly happy to leave the interview to us,' said Marshall. 'Certainly, in the initial stages of the inquiry.'

'If you ask me, having all those journalists outside your front door has spooked you, and you've arrested me to make it look as if you're doing something useful.' Grace looked at the detectives. 'Am I right?'

'I can assure you that is not the case,' said Larch.

However, he was acutely conscious that he was losing control of the situation. He knew that a very different Henry Grace would be facing them were he to be confronted by the brooding presence of Jack Harris. The inspector's absence had given Grace confidence to challenge the detectives.

'This whole thing is preposterous,' said Grace, looking to his solicitor for support. 'I will be taking this further. It just so happens that the chief constable is a good friend of mine. We play golf together. And I do the accounts for his wife's florists as a personal favour to him as well. Did you know that?'

The detectives looked at him bleakly.

'Might I suggest,' said the lawyer, noticing their discomfort, 'that there is a way out of this impasse and that you bail my client until you have something more definite?'

'I am not sure we can do that,' said Larch. 'Your client told me last night that he had had an argument with Dennis McGuffin.'

'Me and the whole world,' snorted Grace. 'The man was a right royal pain in the arse.'

'Henry…' began the lawyer.

'Well, he was, and I don't mind saying it. The fact that he's dead doesn't change the fact that he was a pompous so-an-so but, just because I told him what I thought of him, doesn't mean I murdered the silly old fool. If you follow that line of thinking, you'd have to arrest everyone on the allotments who had received a letter.'

'Yes, but…' said Larch.

'Besides, I told you I was at home all last night. My wife can confirm it.' Grace shot the detectives a sly look. 'We watched a Miss Marple.'

Larch sighed.

'Perhaps,' he said to the lawyer, 'bail might not be a bad idea, after all.'

Chapter fourteen

'Thomas Oldroyd?' said the Reverend Jim Miles in a hollow voice. 'Here? In Levton Bridge?'

'Here,' nodded Harris. 'He's at the station and he wants to see you. Says that you know each other.'

They were sitting in the office at St Cuthbert's, a small room whose walls were adorned with a mixture of religious prints and church notices, some with yellow post-it notes appended to them. Anne Gerrard was working at her desk in the corner of the room, tapping on her computer keyboard even though Jack Harris could see that it was just for show and that she was really listening to every word of the conversation.

There was a tension in the room, a sense of things unsaid, and the inspector noted, as with the previous evening, that the clergyman seemed weighed down by his cares. Harris decided again to give him the time that he needed to compose his thoughts.

'What does he want?' asked the vicar eventually. 'And how come you're talking to me about him? Is it about the murder?'

'Thomas Oldroyd was arrested this morning, and it's two murders now, Jim. Dennis McGuffin's body was found nailed to a tree in a wood not far from here a couple of hours ago.'

The vicar closed his eyes and Anne Gerrard emitted a small gasp.

'Are you alright, Mrs Gerrard?' asked Harris.

She nodded but her face was pale, and the inspector noticed that her right hand was gripping the edge of the desk so hard that the knuckles glowed white; he wondered if she was about to faint but did not move to help her. He had long since learnt that pressure was a valuable investigative tool. The inspector let the silence lengthen.

'I'll be alright,' she said at last. She reached for her bottle of water on the desk and took a drink. 'It's just such a shock. Are you sure it's Dennis?'

'We are, yes. We believe that he may have been abducted from his home after the row at the church last night. I take it that you know nothing about that?'

'I don't think either of us saw him after the argument,' said the vicar. Anne Gerrard nodded her agreement. 'I take it you believe that the two murders are connected?'

'We believe so, yes.' Harris looked at the prints hanging on the wall, one of them depicting Jesus on a cross that was bathed in a shaft of bright sunlight. 'There are strong religious themes to both of them.'

'And where does Thomas Oldroyd fit into this?' asked the clergyman. 'Why have you arrested him?'

'He turned up this morning at the farmhouse that the Lighting the Way people were renting. They left suddenly following the argument last night and we would very much like to talk to them. Do you know where they might have gone?'

Clergyman and secretary exchanged glances.

'No,' said the vicar. 'We did not even know that they had gone. This is awful. Surely, though, you do not believe that Thomas Oldroyd could have anything to do with the murders?'

'He's adamant that he hasn't.'

'Then why have you arrested him? And what does he want with me?'

'He says he wants to confess to an incident that happened in Leicester six months ago.'

'Ravensdale Road,' said the vicar in a flat voice.

'That's the one. He says that he will only talk to you, Jim. Before I agree to his request, though, I need to know what the connection is between you and Thomas Oldroyd.'

The vicar looked at Anne Gerrard.

'Do you want me to go?' she said, standing up. 'If it'll make it easier for you.'

'No, I think you had better stay.' The clergyman gave her an unhappy look then turned his attention to Harris again. 'I am afraid that I have not been completely straight with you, Chief Inspector. *We* have not been completely straight with you.'

'People rarely are, Jim. I usually find out in the end, though, so perhaps now would be a good time to tell me what you know about what has happened.' Harris sat back in his chair. 'You can start with Thomas Oldroyd because I am getting nowhere with him. He just keeps spouting religious gobbledegook. I take it he is telling the truth when he says that you know him?'

'I do know him, yes.' The vicar glanced at his secretary again. 'Anne knows him much better than I do, though.'

'How come?' asked Harris.

Anne seemed unwilling to answer the question. The vicar did it for her.

'We met him through Lighting the Way,' he said. 'We attended some of their prayer meetings when they were in Leicester. That's where I was living when I gave up my job to train for the priesthood.'

'And you?' said Harris, looking at Anne Gerrard. 'Did you go to their meetings as well?'

'I was a member,' she said. 'I still am.'

'Are you now?' Harris leaned forward in his chair, the ramifications playing out in his mind. 'So, which one of you invited them up here then? Who's responsible for all the trouble there's been at St Cuthbert's?'

Both the vicar and his secretary hesitated.

'Dennis can't hurt you now,' said Harris. 'He's off finding out if everything you preach from the pulpit is right, Jim. If you're right, he'll be on his way through the Pearly Gates as we speak. So I ask again, who invited them up here?'

'Neither of us,' said the vicar. 'They followed us after the trouble in Leicester. They wanted to get away from Oldroyd. Neither of us meant for it to happen. We were as surprised as anyone when they turned up at the farm.'

'How did you meet them in the first place?' asked Harris.

'It was at one of their prayer events,' said Anne. Her face assumed a wistful expression. 'On a hill near the city one summer's evening a couple of years ago. It was magical. I'd been brought up as a traditional churchgoer but when I heard Thomas Oldroyd speak, something changed deep within me...' Her voice tailed off; the dreamy expression remained.

'Speak? Was he the leader?' asked Harris. 'I thought it was this David Fulton fellow?'

'Lighting the Way do not believe in hierarchies, Chief Inspector,' said the vicar. 'Everyone is equal before the Lord in their eyes but it is true that Thomas was the most inspirational of them. The man is a fine orator. Something takes hold of him when he addresses an audience. Anne's right, when Thomas Oldroyd spoke, you found your faith reaffirmed.'

'And how come you were there at these gatherings, Jim?' asked Harris. 'Presumably, you were undergoing your training for the priesthood at the time? Wasn't there a clash of cultures?'

'There was, yes, but I'd been aware of Lighting the Way before I sought ordination. I wasn't a member but I've always been drawn to the evangelical movement. I suppose I harboured the belief that the traditional church would be more accepting.' The vicar's voice hardened. 'Dennis McGuffin disavowed me of that notion pretty quickly.'

'He detested Jim,' said Anne, her voice fierce. 'Every time he tried to change something, Dennis would block it, and he took the others with him – none of them had the bottle to stand up for themselves and say what they really thought. Just nodded their agreement. I think Henry Grace was more open to new ideas but he was intimidated by Dennis McGuffin as well. I hated Dennis, Chief Inspector, absolutely hated him and I'm glad he's dead!'

'Now, now, Anne,' said the vicar. He shot her a warning look. 'We should not speak ill of anyone and certainly not of those who have passed into the next realm; God rest his soul.'

'I don't care what happens to his bloody soul, Jim! It can burn in the fires of Hell, for all I care! Lighting the Way offered this church something beautiful, and he destroyed it!'

The vicar stared at her in shocked silence, startled by the venom with which she had spoken, then looked quickly at the detective.

'I am sure she did not mean that,' he said.

'Well, it sounded pretty heartfelt to me,' said Harris. He eyed Anne with renewed interest. 'You seem to carry a lot of anger with you, Mrs Gerrard. Tell me, where were you last night? After the row in the church?'

The vicar looked at the inspector with a beseeching expression on his face.

'You cannot think that Anne was involved in any of this,' he said. 'Surely, there is no need to…'

'It sounds as if she had plenty of reason to see Dennis harmed, Jim, and in murder investigations motive is all.'

The inspector gave the clergyman a stern look. 'We believe that there were two killers. Where were you last night?'

'Oh, come on, this is ridiculous!' exclaimed the vicar.

'Ridiculous or not, I'd still like an answer. Where did you go after the row, Jim? I didn't come to see you until ten so that's at least two hours unaccounted for. Where did you go, what did you do?'

'I'd rather not answer that,' said the vicar, glancing at his secretary.

'Oh, tell him,' she said. 'It's bound to come out sometime. We were together, Chief Inspector. Here.'

'Doing?'

'I don't think...' began the vicar.

'Having sex.' She gave the inspector a devilish look. 'Satisfied? I left a few minutes before you arrived.'

The vicar closed his eyes and Harris raised an eyebrow.

'And how long has this being going on?' asked the inspector.

'A year, eighteen months,' said the vicar with a heavy sigh. 'We met at a Lighting the Way prayer meeting in Leicester.'

'And Tony?' asked Harris, looking at Anne. 'Does he know?'

'No, he doesn't.' Anne gave a mirthless laugh. 'That's one piece of news he hasn't reported on. Too busy with his blessed newspaper to care what I'm doing, is Tony.'

'So, all this stuff about coming up to Levton Bridge to be near your parents, that was just a cover?'

'It's partly true, but Jim was the main reason.'

'And what about Dennis McGuffin?' asked Harris. 'Did he know about your relationship? Because the more I sit here, the more I think that you two, above all people, had reason to see him silenced.'

'No, he did not know,' said the vicar vehemently. 'And to suggest we are involved in this awful business is appalling.'

'But, presumably, you knew John Halstead as well?'

'Yes, we did but…'

'Even though last night you said that you didn't,' said Harris. 'You can see why I'm suspicious, can't you, Jim? It's an old failing of mine when people lie to me.'

The vicar gave the inspector a sick look, and Anne Gerrard stared out of the window. Harris let the silence lengthen as they considered the implications of what he had said.

'We weren't involved in the murders,' said the vicar in a quiet voice eventually. He looked at his secretary. 'We would never do something like that. All we want to do is to live in peace.'

'Oddly enough, that's what Thomas Oldroyd said,' commented the inspector. He stood up and lifted his coat off the back of his chair. 'And he's sitting in one of my cells waiting to confess to assaulting a man who is now dead. Funny old world, isn't it?'

Harris gestured to the door.

'Shall we?' he said.

Chapter fifteen

Alison Butterfield and James Larch arrived at the offices of the Roxham Herald shortly before 1pm.

'I hope this goes better than my interview with Henry Grace,' said Larch gloomily as the officers waited in Reception. 'He's already threatening to report me to Curtis. Says I overstepped my authority.'

'You're only doing your job,' said Butterfield. 'No one can carpet you for that.'

'He plays golf with the Chief Constable.'

'Ah.'

A young woman emerged from the newsroom, gestured to them and the detectives were ushered past the journalists' desks into a cramped office with walls largely covered by untidily stacked bookshelves. Tony Gerrard was sitting behind his desk, dressed smartly in a dark suit and tie. However, unlike the previous evening, it seemed to Butterfield that the editor was less relaxed, more guarded, as he watched the detectives enter the room.

'I did not expect to see you again so soon,' he said, looking at Butterfield. He motioned for the officers to take a seat. 'Is it about the murders?'

'It is, yes,' said Butterfield as the detectives sat down.

'It's dramatic stuff,' said Gerrard. 'However, like I said last night, I'm not sure I can help you. I told you everything I could.'

'Not everything,' said Butterfield.

Gerrard eyed the detectives uneasily as Butterfield took the print-out of the Leicester Standard news story from her coat pocket, holding it up so that the editor could see it.

'You wrote this, I think?' she said. 'About the incident in Ravensdale Road.'

Tony Gerrard looked closer and gave a laugh that sounded false. Forced.

'Boy, that's going back a while,' he said. 'Hardly my finest piece of journalism. Not exactly going to win the Pulitzer Prize.'

'But you *did* write it?'

'Yes. Not long before I left the Leicester Standard but why would you be interested in a piddling little story like that? Surely, it's got nothing to do with the murders?'

'Lighting the Way might have,' said Larch.

'Oh, come off it!' exclaimed Gerrard. 'They may be a bunch of cranks, but they're harmless enough.'

'Are they?' Larch gave the journalist a hard look. 'This is not to be made public yet, and certainly not in your newspaper, but we think that the man assaulted in Ravensdale Road was the guy found dead on the allotment last night. We now think that he's not called Michael Hills but John Halstead – and we think that you may be able to tell us what he was doing up here.'

'Why me?'

'You wrote this.' Butterfield held up the print-out.

'Yes, but I told you last night that I don't know him.' Gerrard tried to appear unconcerned, but beads of sweat glistened on his forehead. 'And I have absolutely no idea why he was using our house name. There really is no connection with me or the Roxham Herald.'

'And yet,' said Butterfield, tapping the print out, 'you were the only journalist to report on the incident in Ravensdale Road. We are wondering how you found out about it?'

'I'm not sure I remember.'

'You'll have to do better than that, Mr Gerrard.'

'I wrote hundreds of stories when I was on the Standard. Thousands, probably. I can't be expected to remember where they all came from. I imagine I got this one from a police press release.'

'Leicester police did not issue a press release,' said Larch. 'So, how *did* you find out about it?'

'A journalist has his contacts.' The reply sounded evasive and Gerard avoided eye contact with the officers. Instead, he seemed fascinated by the need to tidy up a sheaf of papers sitting on his desk.

'And who was your contact on this one?' asked Butterfield. 'Who tipped you off?'

'A journalist has a duty to protect his informants, just like you do. Some journalists have even gone to jail to protect the people who give them information.'

'That's a thought worth bearing in mind,' said Butterfield. She enjoyed the anxiety that flickered across the editor's face. 'You do know that I could arrest you for obstructing our inquiries, I take it? Do you think that would make the front page? Better than, what did you call it last night, some twaddle about the public toilets in Market Place?'

'Now hang on a minute!'

'However,' said Butterfield, giving him a reassuring smile, 'I am sure it will not come to that. All I want to know is where you got the information. It's not as if it's a major story. This isn't Watergate. We're not looking for Deep Throat here.'

Gerrard looked at the unyielding expression on the detective constable's face and sighed.

'My wife,' he said. 'OK? The story came from Anne. The police press office didn't know anything about it when I rang them, so I went on what Anne told me. She wasn't very happy about what I had done. We had a fearful row about it.'

'And how did *she* know about what happened?' asked Larch.

'I'd rather not say.'

'Might I remind you that this is a murder investigation?' said Larch. 'And when people start acting evasively, we get to thinking that they've got something to hide. *Have* you got something to hide, Mr Gerrard?'

Gerrard gave the detectives a defeated look.

'OK, OK,' he said, holding up his hands. 'She knew about it because she is a member of Lighting the Way and she was there at Ravensdale Road when it happened.'

The detectives looked at each other, sensing that a routine conversation was about to assume much more significance.

'So, she must have known John Halstead then?' said Butterfield slowly.

A pause. A heavy sigh.

'She did, yes.'

'And you – did you know him?'

'I never met any of them,' said Gerrard. 'They're not my type. In fact, I had loads of arguments with Anne about her knocking about with them. I wanted her to stop.'

'Why?' asked Larch.

'They're soft in the head, if you ask me.' There was a new energy to the editor's voice. A passion that had been masked behind the barriers. 'All this mumbo jumbo about faith being able to do anything, it got right up my nose. She's always been a bit gullible has my wife, and she lapped it all up. Absolutely lapped it up. Even gave them money.'

'How much?'

'Just a couple of hundred but I knew that would just be the start.' Gerrard gave a mirthless laugh. 'They may say that the Good Lord provides for their needs but it rather hides the fact that it's social security that actually pays the bills. That and donations from weak-minded people like my wife. As someone who works all hours, that really sticks in my craw.'

'How serious were the tensions between the two of you?' asked Larch.

'Serious enough. We were fine until they started to fill her head with all that rubbish. We were even talking about starting a family but once the arguments started, Anne did not want to know. I tell you, she believed everything they said. I didn't get a look in.'

'So, do we take it that your wife was the person responsible for Lighting the Way coming up north then?' asked Butterfield.

'I'd rather that did not become public knowledge.'

'Why be so secretive? They may be a bit wacky but surely it's nothing to be ashamed of?'

'Think it through,' replied Gerrard. 'Anne manages the office at St Cuthbert's and they've been trying to find out who invited them for ages. Dennis McGuffin asks her every day if she has heard anything. He's convinced that them coming up here was down to the vicar. He's has been angling for a reason to sack him ever since he arrived but, if he thought that Anne was the reason Lighting the Way were here, he'd fire her instead and we need the money. Being editor of the Roxham Herald is hardly the best paid job in the world.'

'Well, I shouldn't worry about Dennis McGuffin,' said Butterfield.

Gerrard looked at her keenly.

'Rumour has it he's one of the murder victims,' he said. 'You going to confirm that in return for all my help? A nice exclusive?'

'I am afraid not,' replied Butterfield. 'Your wife was the one who invited Lighting the Way up here then?'

'Not in as many words. After the incident at Ravensdale Road, several of the group were frightened that it might happen again and wanted to get out of Leicester. They knew Jim Miles – he'd been to some of their prayer meetings – and when he asked Anne if she wanted a job at St Cuthbert's, the Lighting the Way people thought the area sounded nice and decided to follow her. They reckoned they would be made welcome.'

'But they weren't,' said Butterfield.

'No, they weren't. People in this area are very narrow-minded. Very set in their ways.'

'So folks keep telling me,' said the constable, thinking of Matty Gallagher.

'You should see what I get sent for the letters column.' Gerrard reached for a pile of hand-written papers and held them up. 'Half of it goes straight in the bin. They've clearly never heard of the libel laws up here. There's not a lot of tolerance going on in this valley. Mind you, I don't blame them when it comes to Lighting the Way. I have very little time for them either.'

'So how did you feel when they followed your wife here?' asked Larch.

'How do you think I bloody felt?' said the editor bitterly. 'I hoped it would be a new start for us, close to her parents and without David Fulton and his pals whispering in her ear every minute of the day. I thought that she would forget about them and we could maybe start talking about having a kid again. Then they turned up out of the blue. I was pretty angry.'

'Angry enough to kill?' asked Larch.

The editor stared at him in disbelief.

'What, you think that I…?' He did not finish the sentence.

'We have to check,' said Butterfield. 'Where you were between eight and nine last night? Before myself and Sergeant Gallagher came here to see you?'

'At home.'

'Anyone verify that?' asked Butterfield.

'No, Anne was at some sort of church meeting then she went out with a friend for a drink and did not get back until past ten.' Gerrard looked anxious, and a muscle beneath his right eye started to twitch. 'Look, if you really think that I could be capable of committing a murder you'd better think...'

'Do you know a man called Thomas Oldroyd?' asked Larch.

Gerrard looked even more worried. Frightened even, thought Larch.

'Why do you want to know about him?' he asked.

'Just answer the question, Mr Gerrard.'

'I've never met him, no.'

'But you do know who he is?' Larch fixed the journalist with a hard stare. 'You might as well tell us; we'll find out in the end.'

Gerrard sighed.

'OK, OK,' he said. 'Anne said that he was the man who tried to force his way into the house in Ravensdale Road.'

'And why would he do that?'

'He'd been one of their members but there was some form of falling out. They tried to get him to leave. Listen, if Thomas Oldroyd is in this area, I want me and Anne kept out of this. The man's a nutjob. He's threatened several of the Lighting the Way folks since they left Leicester.'

Larch glanced at Butterfield. This was getting better and better.

'Threatened how?' he asked.

'Sent them texts. Saying that it wasn't over. That he'd be back. Anne got a couple of them. Frightening, they were.'

'She still got them?' asked Larch.

'No, she deleted them and blocked his number. Do you think he's behind the murders?'

James Larch smiled. Much better than the interview with Henry Grace, he decided.

Chapter sixteen

The Reverend Jim Miles waited a long time at the far end of the corridor leading to the interview room at Levton Bridge Police Station as he summoned the courage to take his next step. Harris stood a few feet away and dispassionately surveyed the vicar's bloodless cheeks as the clergyman leaned against the wall and closed his eyes.

'You alright?' asked Harris.

The inspector tried to sound liked he cared but his patience was fast running out with a man he considered to be a weak character of dubious moral fibre – and one protecting more secrets than he had divulged so far. Indeed, Harris had only agreed to let Jim Miles sit in on the interview with Thomas Oldroyd in the hope that it would increase the pressure on the clergyman's fragile mind and loosen his tongue even further.

The vicar gave him a wan look.

'I am not feeling very well,' he said. 'I really do not wish to do this. Can we do it another time?'

'We all have to do things we don't want to do, Reverend. I'd rather be up on the hills with the dogs but that's not going to happen.'

'You're different, though, Chief Inspector. You're used to confronting situations like this.'

'Not that different,' said Harris. 'We both confront evil in our jobs, do we not? It comes with the territory. Surely, they taught you that at theological college? Satan striding across the planet, dispensing evil wherever he goes?'

'They did not teach us about situations like this.' The vicar leaned more heavily against the wall. 'They couldn't prepare us for someone like Thomas Oldroyd. No one could.'

'What does he have over you?'

'Nothing. Why?' Miles sounded guarded. 'What could he possibly have over me?'

'You seem reluctant to meet him. Frightened even. A lot of people seem to feel the same way about him.'

'You don't know him. He is wicked.'

'Nothing I have seen today has led me to think that Thomas Oldroyd is wicked, Jim.'

'Well, he is. A wicked man, a truly wicked man!' The vigour of the outburst surprised the inspector, the vicar's words coming in a rush as he took a step forward and stared at the inspector with wide eyes. 'And one not to be trusted. Don't believe anything he says. It's all lies. All of it. Lies!'

'Pot or kettle, Jim?'

The comment drained the energy from the clergyman and he leaned against the wall again.

'Besides,' said Harris, 'Thomas has been calm and courteous throughout, and he seems genuinely penitent about what happened at Ravensdale Road. That's why he wants to see you. To seek absolution.'

'Absolution,' snorted the vicar. 'That's a laugh. You didn't see him that night. He was out of control. He's got a terrible temper.'

Harris looked sharply at him.

'I thought you said that you weren't there,' he said.

The vicar sighed.

'I lied,' he said. 'I was there.'

'As you so rightly said last night, sometimes it can be difficult to work out where the evil lies.' Harris glared at him. 'I have to say that you have given a very poor account of yourself. Do they teach you deceit at theological college or does it come naturally?'

'Now, hang on, just because…'

'Why were you in Ravensdale Road?'

The vicar hesitated, but the inspector's piercing stare broke down the last of his resistance.

'I was with Anne,' he said quietly. 'I saw it all. Saw what Thomas Oldroyd is like.'

'For fuck's sake, Jim, why do you keep doing this? You do know that this is a murder inquiry, I take it? That I could arrest you for withholding evidence – you and Anne?'

'Yes, I know, but we were worried that admitting my true links with Lighting the Way would jeopardise my job if Dennis McGuffin found out.'

'And lying your head off doesn't?' exclaimed Harris. 'Jesus, man, you're supposed to be providing moral guidance.'

'Nobody's perfect.'

'You could at least make an effort.'

The vicar looked at him unhappily.

'This has been a very testing time for me,' he said.

'Not as testing as it has been for the two men lying in the mortuary with masonry nails driven into their skulls,' said Harris. 'Anything else before we go in there? Any more little surprises to look forward to?'

'No, no, nothing. Honest.'

'There's a word that's been devalued today,' said Harris. 'If you're lying again, Jim, so help me, you'll be lucky if they let you collect up the bibles after Sunday service by the time I have finished with you.'

'It won't be me lying. Thomas Oldroyd is a fantasist. Lives in a world of his own.'

Harris did not reply and they walked down the corridor and into the interview room where Matty Gallagher was waiting, sitting opposite Oldroyd, who gave a half smile when he saw the clergyman.

'The Reverend Miles, as I live and breathe,' he said. 'Who would have thought it after all these months?'

'Thomas,' said the vicar sitting down and eying him nervously. 'I understand you want to see me?'

'Has he told you?' asked Oldroyd, looking at Harris.

'Told me what?' asked the inspector. He took a seat next to Oldroyd.

'That he stole my woman.'

Harris glowered at the vicar.

'I thought you said you told me everything,' he said.

'I didn't mention it because he's deluded,' replied Miles vehemently. 'Anne was never with him.'

'She loved me,' said Oldroyd. 'She still does.'

'No, she doesn't.' Miles looked at Harris with a beseeching look on his face. 'She never loved him. I told you, he's a fantasist, Jack.'

'It seems to be mandatory for you religious types, and it's Chief Inspector Harris to you, Reverend. To be honest, I'm not really bothered about your sordid love lives. I'm more interested in my dead bodies. Thomas, you said you would talk to me if a priest was in the room.'

'Yes, well, I won't. I only wanted to see him again.'

'I've had just about enough of this!' snapped Harris. 'Tell me what happened with John Halstead at Ravensdale Road, or so help me, I'll charge you with obstructing my inquiries. Do you fancy a night in the cells?'

Oldroyd considered the comment for a few moments then shook his head.

'I'll talk,' he said, 'but I had nothing to do with the murders, although after I tell you what happened at

Ravensdale Road, I imagine that you might think differently.'

'Why did you go there?' asked Gallagher.

'To confront David Fulton and the others. Get them to see what had really been happening.'

'And what had been happening?'

'Halstead had poisoned them against me and David had turned the others against me.' Oldroyd nodded at the vicar. 'Including him and Anne. None of them would talk to me. They thought I was making it all up. I went back to the house to try to convince them that I was right about John Halstead.'

'What about him?'

'That he wasn't the friend they all thought he was. That he was seeking to undermine everything that we were trying to achieve with Lighting the Way.'

'Undermine how?' asked Gallagher.

'How much do you know about him?'

'Not much really,' admitted the sergeant. 'He is proving somewhat elusive to pin down. We do know that he used at least three names and pretended to be a journalist.'

'At least that last bit is true. He *was* a journalist. He worked on the Roxham Herald as a trainee years ago.'

'Are you sure?' asked Harris.

'That's what I heard. I don't think he was there long then he went somewhere in the Midlands, the Derby Standard, I think. Sometime in the mid-Nineties.'

'If he started at Roxham, it explains why he knew about the name Michael Hills,' said Gallagher. He looked at Harris, who nodded. The sergeant returned his attention to Oldroyd. 'We were wondering if all the false names meant that John Halstead was some sort of conman. Scamming people, maybe.'

'John Halstead earned his money by being a private investigator. One that was determined to bring down Lighting the Way.'

'That's a lie!' exclaimed the Reverend Miles. 'John Halstead was a good man. He believed totally in what we were trying to do and your suggestion that he was trying to undermine us is abhorrent. I told you, Jack… Chief Inspector… the man's a fantasist. I didn't believe it when he claimed it in Leicester, and I don't believe it now.'

Harris looked at the clergyman without much enthusiasm.

'So, you knew about this as well then?' he said coldly. 'Knew that he was investigating the group?'

'I knew what Thomas was saying, yes, but I didn't mention it because it's a pack of lies and if you know what's good for…'

'Sergeant,' said Harris, looking at Gallagher, 'would you be so good as to escort the Reverend to a cell, please? Thomas, are you prepared to keep talking to us if he goes?'

Oldroyd gave a sly smile.

'I suppose so,' he said. 'I just wanted to see him squirm.'

Gallagher stood up and gestured for the stunned vicar to follow him out of the room.

'This is outrageous!' gasped Miles.

'So is repeatedly lying to a murder investigation,' replied Harris. 'Criminally outrageous, in fact. Sergeant, tell Custody that we are holding the Reverend Miles on suspicion of obstructing our inquiries, will you?'

'Be my pleasure,' said Gallagher. He took hold of the vicar's arm. 'Come on.'

The dazed clergyman stood unsteadily to his feet and allowed the sergeant to lead him from the room.

'Now, where were we?' asked the inspector when they had gone. 'Ah, yes, John Halstead. What was he investigating?'

'He made his money investigating religious cults then selling the information to whoever would pay the most for it. Earned a nice living, from what I heard. Sometimes it was a newspaper; sometimes it was the police.'

'The police?'

'Sometimes, yes. He'd go on their list of informers. He'd been doing it for years. All over the country.'

'How do I know you're telling the truth?' asked Harris.

'People may accuse me of many things but dishonesty is not one of them.'

'Nevertheless…'

'Besides, there's a way that you can check. Do you remember that big story a few years ago about a religious cult in Manchester? A couple and their daughter kept three young girls prisoner in a house in the city. One of the girls hadn't been out for four years. Your lot found her chained to a bed.'

'I remember it,' said Harris. The house had been raided in the weeks before he left CID at Greater Manchester Police to take up his posting at Levton Bridge. 'In fact, I know some of the officers who were involved in the investigation.'

'In which case, they can confirm that a lot of the information they used to prosecute them came from John Halstead. He spent six months infiltrating the group then sold the story to one of the redtops and police arrested the leaders after it appeared in the paper.'

'But surely what he was doing was laudable? I don't agree with selling stories to the press before the police can investigate but his motives were good, weren't they?'

'It depends if you think living purely for material gain is a good thing, Chief Inspector,' said Oldroyd. 'Personally, I don't. Just look at my father. He sold out every principle that he ever had and all for money. When I was a kid he thought more of his latest new car than he did me. Besides, John Halstead's motives were not always good. Money corrupted him. The man became a mercenary. Like my father.'

'Meaning?'

'Meaning that, after what happened in Manchester, Halstead needed another target pretty damn quick and he settled on Lighting the Way. Charmed his way in.'

'Why select Lighting the Way?'

'He claimed that Neil Harker and his girlfriend had been brainwashed by us. I'm not sure that he believed it, though. If you ask me, he was just looking for an easy payday.'

'Did you tell him that?'

'Not at first. I wanted to be sure so I rang up a friend of mine who knew what he had done in Manchester – and no, I won't tell you his name. When I told him what Halstead looked like, it became clear that it was the same man. Lighting the Way is no cult, Chief Inspector. They may be a bit naïve but their instincts are basically good.'

'So, people keep telling me,' said Harris. 'So, you went to the house in Ravensdale Road to try and get Halstead kicked out of the group? Get yourself back in?'

'Something like that. Trouble is, when I got there, Halstead tried to stop me talking to them.'

'And you lost your temper?'

'I am afraid so.' Oldroyd shook his head. 'I struck him on the face. Unforgivable. Absolutely unforgivable.'

'You'll struggle to get much in the way of absolution then.'

'Maybe among men but the Lord forgives all sins.'

'Very convenient, Thomas,' said Harris. 'Besides, your sinning didn't stop there, did it? You went back for more the next evening? In the pub?'

'I did, yes. It was a silly thing to do, but I was furious that they wouldn't listen to me. They were blinded to the truth.'

'*Your* truth, maybe. Only this time Halstead struck you, I think?'

Oldroyd lifted a hand to his cheek as if he could still feel the pain from the blow.

'Yes,' he said quietly. 'Yes, he did.'

'And how did that make you feel?'

'Shocked.'

'We suspect it made you feel a bit more than that,' said the inspector. 'We think it made you so angry that, after Lighting the Way left Leicester, you tracked them up here and killed John Halstead in revenge.'

'Like I said, Chief Inspector, I did not kill anyone.'

'Why were you at the farm this morning?'

'There was much unfinished between me and the others, but I was not there to harm them.' He sat back in his seat. 'I am seeking forgiveness for attacking John Halstead in Leicester and nothing else. That's the only thing I'll admit to having done. What will happen to me now?'

Harris stood up.

'You'll be held on suspicion of the assault at Ravensdale Road,' he said. 'The detective from Leicester will be here soon, and she'll want to talk to you about it. It's her call on whether or not you are charged.'

'And the murders?'

'I'm not sure at this stage, Thomas.' Harris headed for the door then turned back. 'Tell me, do you know anything about a man purporting to be John Halstead who died in a car crash a couple of days after the incident in the pub?'

Oldroyd shook his head.

'I am afraid not,' he said with a slight smile. 'I only know of two men who was raised from the dead to live again – and neither Lazarus or our risen Lord Jesus Christ could drive.'

Harris nodded gloomily and left the room. He had only gone a few steps down the corridor when a uniformed officer approached him.

'You've got a visitor,' said the officer, not even trying to conceal the smile.

'Don't tell me, it's the deranged Edie Prentice?' said Harris sourly.

'No,' chuckled the officer, 'it's the deranged Henry Grace. Said something about an official complaint. I've never seen him angry. He's spitting feathers.'

'That's all I need.' Harris sighed. 'Where have you put the mad old chuff?'

* * *

A couple of minutes later, the inspector pushed his way into the interview room off the reception area.

'Henry,' said the inspector, taking a seat and trying to strike an affable tone, 'and what brings you here, as if I didn't know?'

'I want to know what the hell you are playing at!' exclaimed Grace angrily. Flecks of spittle flew from his mouth. 'I expected better of you! I am a respectable citizen; you know that, and yet I have been accused of murder by your pups.'

'Scoot and Archie been up to no good then?'

Grace looked baffled.

'Sorry,' said Harris, 'bad joke. They're my dogs.'

'This is no time for joking man! I am referring to those two young detectives you sent to interview me. Accusing me of murder! I have never heard of anything so ridiculous in all my life. I have a reputation in this community.'

'I am sure they did not actually accuse you of…'

'They didn't need to! The implication was clear enough. Like, if I wanted to kill Dennis McGuffin, I'd be stupid enough as to do it in the middle of his onion patch!'

Harris thought of Matty Gallagher. Tried to resist the temptation. Failed dismally.

'Actually,' said the inspector, 'I'm told by my sergeant that it's a bit late in the year for onions.'

Henry Grace stared at him in astonishment then opened his mouth to reply.

Chapter seventeen

Suitably harangued, Jack Harris ushered Henry Grace out of the interview room and down the police station steps. When he was sure that Grace had gone, an ill-tempered DCI walked back across the reception area and pushed his way through the back office door to see Matty Gallagher approaching along the corridor.

'Trouble in Paradise?' asked the sergeant on seeing the DCI's thunderous expression.

'Just Henry Grace banging on,' said Harris as the detectives fell into step and started to climb the stairs to the first floor. 'Reckons that we have infringed his civil rights.'

'Those pesky old things, eh?'

'Talking of civil rights, how's his Most High Reverence? Settling into his new home?'

'He was blubbing like a baby when I left him in the cell,' replied Gallagher. He frowned. 'I've asked the custody sergeant to keep an eye on him.'

'You worried that he might do something stupid?'

'Not sure. His faith certainly does not seem to be offering him much in the way of sustenance. He said that his Lord had forsaken him in his hour of need.' They reached the top of the stairs. 'That's when he started crying.'

'God knows how he got the job.'

'I imagine he does,' said Gallagher. He waited for a reaction. 'It must have been a good interview. Be a bit like being interviewed by you, I imagine. Just less scary.'

'Yes, very droll, Sergeant.'

'I'm wasted on you, I really am,' said Gallagher. 'This is my best material, you know.'

'Really?'

'Really,' grinned Gallagher. 'You serious about charging the vicar with obstruction then?'

'I've got half a mind to.' The officers entered the inspector's office to be greeted enthusiastically by the dogs, all slaver and furiously wagging tails. 'Jim Miles has lied to us right from the off, and I have this feeling that there may be more to come from him.'

'Me, too. I can't quite put my finger on it but there's something not right about the man.' Gallagher reached down to scratch Scoot behind the ear, then took a seat at the desk. 'He's not like any vicar I've ever known.'

'And that's a lot, is it? We an expert in the clergy, are we?'

'No, not really,' admitted Gallagher. 'Haven't been to church since I was a nipper. Julie's parents are big churchgoers, though, and her mum keeps badgering me to go with them to the Methodist chapel down at Roxham, but it's not for me. Do you think Jim Miles could be tied up with the murders somehow?'

'He and his little lady friend certainly had plenty of reason to dislike Dennis McGuffin.' Harris filled up a couple of dog bowls from the kettle. 'Maybe they felt the same about John Halstead as well. He *was* trying to destroy their beloved Lighting the Way, after all.'

'Except Jim Miles told you that no one believed what Thomas Oldroyd was telling them about Halstead. If that's right, then none of the Lighting the Way people had reason to see Halstead harmed. Quite the opposite. He was one of their own. One of the good guys.'

'But Miles could be lying again.' Harris placed the bowls on the floor. 'He does seem to have a distant acquaintance with the truth.'

'Maybe.'

'OK,' said Harris, sitting down at his desk. 'How's this? What if Oldroyd did persuade David Fulton and his friends that Halstead really was up to no good? They would all have a reason to see Halstead and McGuffin harmed then, wouldn't they? And we'd have a bunch of holy warriors riding round the countryside waiting for God to tell them who to kill next.'

'I guess.'

'Which is why we have to find that minibus. And find it soon. And whichever officers catch up with them will have to be careful. These people could be dangerous.'

Matty Gallagher did not reply.

* * *

Shortly before 1.30pm, the motorway patrol car pulled into the service station off the busy southbound carriageway of the M6 near Preston, just as the sun burst through the clouds and a shaft of light bathed the site in a soft glow. As the driver cut the engine, he glanced across at the battered minibus parked nearby and recalled something he had read in that day's briefing notes.

'You got the registration number for that minibus they were looking for up in Cumbria?' he asked his partner.

'Somewhere.' She pulled a sheaf of papers from the side pocket of the door, flicked through the pages then checked the number they had been given against the plate on the minibus. 'That's it alright. Good spot. Can't see anyone inside, mind.'

'Maybe they've stopped for a coffee.' The officer looked across to the service station. 'What do we know about them?'

'Some kind of religious group. Two men, two women. All fairly young. Two of them are teenagers. They're wanted for questioning by a DCI Harris at Levton Bridge. It's a nasty one. The dead guys were crucified. One of them was nailed to a shed on an allotment.'

'Hotbeds of bad blood are allotments,' said her colleague.

'Really?' She looked doubtful. 'Allotments?'

'Oh, aye,' he said. 'Hotbeds. I had one a few years ago and blokes were always falling out over boundary fences.'

'Best call in some back-up then,' said his accomplice with a slight smile.

* * *

Jack Harris surveyed his sergeant intently across the desk. The inspector had noted Gallagher's uneasy expression for several minutes, as if the sergeant had something to say but could not quite summon the words. Or maybe did not wish to; Harris knew that he could sometimes be an intimidating presence, even for experienced officers like Matty Gallagher, and although having a reputation often came in useful, the inspector also knew that sometimes it stifled debate.

'Go on, spit it out,' said the inspector.

'Spit what out?'

'Whatever's been bugging you, Matty lad.'

'You know me too well.' Gallagher gave his boss a rueful smile. 'OK, I'm not really buying all this stuff about religious types going round killing each other.'

'I guessed that. Why the doubts?'

'I know that there are strong forces at work here – I do get that, really I do – but I'm just not convinced that any of these people are capable of committing murder. I mean, isn't one of the Ten Commandments "Thou Shalt Not Kill"?'

'It is,' said Harris, 'but if history teaches us anything, it's that human beings are perfectly capable of doing anything if the situation demands.'

'That does not change the fact that I can't see any of the religious people we have dealt with being able to commit murder. Certainly not any of the Lighting the Way lot. I reckon Gillian was right about them all along. Innocents abroad. They're caught up in something that does not really involve them, I'm sure of it.'

'And Jim Miles and Anne Gerrard? Do you include them in that?'

'I am afraid I do. Jim Miles is far too weak to kill anyone.'

'But what if Anne egged him on?' asked Harris. 'He wouldn't be the first man to fall for that one. Sex is as powerful a motive as they come.'

'The old femme fatale routine?' Gallagher shook his head. 'Anne Gerrard flashes a stocking top, and Jim Miles turns from feeble-minded cleric to raging killer? Na, I can't see it. She's not the type to do that.'

'She's capable of being deceitful, though. I mean, she's been going behind her husband's back for eighteen months.'

'It's a big jump from adultery to murder.'

'Granted,' said Harris. He nodded his agreement. 'So, where does Thomas Oldroyd fit into things then?'

'Now he's different,' said the sergeant thoughtfully. 'Of all of them, he's the one who most intrigues me. Dark waters run deep there, I reckon, but even so, I'm still not sure that he could kill anyone. We've not seen any sign of it, have we? I mean, the guy's spent six months beating himself up for slapping John Halstead. Difficult to see him resorting to cold-blooded murder.'

'You're not leaving us much in the way of suspects, Matty lad.'

'Sorry.'

'No need to apologise. I expect my officers to speak up if they think we're getting things wrong, but if you're correct, what's the alternative? Who do we put in the frame instead?'

'Don't shout at me but I don't think that we should be closing our minds to the bad feeling on the allotments quite so readily.'

'I let James bring Henry Grace in.'

'Yes, I know you did, but there's no way that he's our man. I mean, this is Henry Grace we're talking about, for God's sake.'

'Agreed,' said Harris. 'And I'm not sure we handled his situation as well as we could have either. We'll have to smooth things out with him some way. But if not him, then who?'

'According to James, plenty of the other plot-holders had good reason to dislike Dennis McGuffin.'

'Except forensics are adamant that the same people committed both murders, and John Halstead had no connection with the allotments.'

'That we know of. I just can't help feeling that we're missing something here.'

'OK, how about this?' said Harris. He stood up. 'We let Jim Miles and Thomas Oldroyd stew, see if they come up with anything else after a couple of hours in the cells, but we keep looking at the plot holders as well?'

'Sounds like a plan. So, what do we do first?'

'The first thing,' said Harris as he opened his desk drawer and took out two dog leads, 'is to take the hounds for a walk.'

'Not sure that's a good idea, guv. There's still a load of media outside the front. They're bound to clock you heading out, and you don't want a picture of you walking the dogs to appear on the front page of the newspapers, do you? There's a load of freelancers looking for something to flog to the nationals.'

'You're right,' said Harris with a sigh. 'God, I hate the media.'

The inspector looked at the dogs, who were surveying him hopefully, their eyes bright and their ears pricked up.

'Sorry, boys,' he said. 'I am afraid it's twice round the station again. Maybe tomorrow.'

'You hope,' said Gallagher. He also stood up. 'You want me to work with James on the allotment angle then?'

'Sure, but first I want you to have a run down to Roxham to see Tony Gerrard again.'

'And say what?'

'Tell him what we know. Maybe he can shed some light on what John Halstead was doing when he was on the Roxham Herald. It won't take long and, after that, you can link up with James. Who knows, maybe you'll have better luck in persuading Henry Grace not to put in an official complaint. I didn't get anywhere with him.'

'And how hard did you try?' asked Gallagher. He gave the inspector a knowing look.

'Perhaps I was not as diplomatic as I could have been.'

'Get-away with you. OK, I'll see what I can do to calm the old duffer down. What are you going to do after taking the dogs for a walk?'

'I'm going to ring Leckie. See if he can confirm Oldroyd's story about the cult in Manchester.

'Always a good idea,' said Gallagher. 'Everything feels better after a chat with Leckie.'

As the sergeant walked out into the corridor, Philip Curtis entered the room.

'Matthew,' said the commander, nodding at the sergeant as they passed each other. 'Everything OK?'

'Yes, sir,' said Gallagher. 'Making a bit of progress, I think.'

'Good.' The commander sat down at Harris's desk and tried not to scowl as the dogs looked hopefully at him; many staff visiting the office brought treats. 'Sounds promising, Jack? Goodness knows we need something to tell the media. And HQ are getting really twitchy. We need an early arrest on this one.'

'I wish I had Matty's optimistic nature,' replied Harris. 'At the moment all we're doing is ruling people out.'

'Including Henry Grace, I hope.'

'Ah, you heard then.'

'He's rung the Chief's office three times. They're old friends, apparently. What do I tell him?'

'That we apologise but we had to rule him out of our enquiries.'

'So what *do* we have?'

'Matty is convinced that we're missing something that ties all of this together and I tend to agree. None of it makes any sense at the moment and we just keep going round in circles.'

'You not fancy Oldroyd?'

'I don't fancy anyone at this stage, to be honest. Did you come to see me for anything specific?'

'Ah, yes. The media are putting the pressure on us to name the victims. They have already worked out it's Dennis McGuffin – it's the talk of the town – and Tony Gerrard has been onto the press office threatening to name Halstead on his website. Says he can't sit on the information forever. How did he find out?'

'Alison had to tell him. See if he knew the guy, both of them being journalists.'

'Unavoidable, I guess,' said Curtis. 'Any reason I can't tell the press office to name them?'

'Yeah, go for it. Might even help. We are having the same trouble finding anyone related to Halstead that Leicestershire Police had. Assuming, that is, that Halstead was his real name. Anything's possible with this bloke, and we still don't know where he fits into things.'

'We Ok to name McGuffin? Do his relatives know that he's dead? I don't want them hearing about it from the media.'

'Yeah, go for it. His nearest relative is an elderly sister in Bedfordshire. The local cop shop sent someone round to break the news to her but she's got dementia, apparently. Didn't even know who he was. They tracked down a cousin as well.'

Curtis stood up.

'OK,' he said. 'I'll let the press office know.'

'Here's hoping,' said Harris.

* * *

Less than an hour after the minibus had first been sighted in the motorway services car park, a team of uniformed officers cautiously entered the main building. Two of them wore holstered handguns concealed beneath their jackets, and the team fanned out across the concourse, moving in unhurried fashion as they sought out their quarry. It did not take them long to see David Fulton and his friends huddled round a corner table in the Costa coffee area, deep in intense conversation. Fulton was the one doing most of the talking. He was also the first to see the approaching police officers and he gave a startled cry and leapt to his feet. As he did so, a constable walked up quietly behind him and placed a restraining hand on his shoulder.

'Now don't do anything stupid, son,' said the officer calmly. 'We don't want a scene, do we? Not with all these families around.'

Fulton thought for a moment, noticed the children on the next table and nodded. The other Lighting the Way members sat transfixed as they watched the officer pull Fulton's arms behind his back and snap on the handcuffs. Fulton winced with the pain.

'There's no need for that,' he protested as the officer guided him out from behind the table. 'We've done nothing wrong, and you have no right to arrest us.'

'You can tell that to DCI Harris when you get to Levton Bridge,' said the officer. 'I'm sure he'd love to debate the issue of civil rights with you. It's all they talk about up there, apparently.'

Chapter eighteen

Detective Chief Inspector Grant Wayman stood in the squad room in Derby's city centre police station and stared in amazement at the television screen. A burly shaven-headed man in a dark suit, he had investigated numerous murder cases during a twenty-five-year career before being tasked with establishing the city's new Cold Case Review team, and had long since ceased to be surprised by the turns of events that the job routinely threw at him. But even the veteran detective was taken aback by what was unfolding on the screen, as he stood surrounded by a cluster of fellow detectives who all gazed at the television in similar bemusement.

The subject of their interest was a Sky Television reporter who was broadcasting live from outside Levton Bridge Police Station.

'Police confirmed that Mr Halstead's body was found on an allotment on the edge of Levton Bridge at about 8pm last night,' said the reporter, 'and that Mr McGuffin was found in a small wood nine miles to the south of the town early this morning after his car was reported by a member of the public.'

'So much for John Halstead dying in a car crash,' said Wayman sourly. And where the hell is Levton Bridge anyway? Anyone know?'

A couple of the other officers shrugged, and another called up Google on his mobile phone.

'Somewhere in the sticks,' he said, peering at his device. 'The North Pennines, by the looks of it.' He ran his finger across the screen. 'Hey, it's not far from Roxham. Isn't that where Tony Gerrard works?'

'It is indeed,' said Wayman. 'Looks like we're going have to bring things forward. Did Levton Bridge feature in the original investigation?'

'Not that I know of,' said one of the officers. 'There's nothing to link Elaine to that part of the world. The only connection is that Gerrard edits the Roxham Herald.'

Wayman returned his attention to the television.

'Police will not confirm how the men died except to say that this is a murder inquiry,' continued the reporter, 'but sources have told Sky TV that they were crucified.'

'I guess they have to make their own entertainment up there,' said one of the detectives. 'Makes a change from shagging sheep, I suppose.'

A ripple of laughter ran round the room. Wayman gave him a sharp look.

'I want none of that,' he said. 'I want nothing less than total respect shown when we get up there.'

'The investigation is being led by Detective Inspector Jack Harris, who heads up CID in the division,' continued the reporter. Film of Harris addressing the journalists from the top of the police station steps appeared on the screen. 'He has yet to comment on the naming of the victims but earlier in the day police said they believe the crimes are targeted and that the wider public should not be concerned. However, their words have done little to assuage local concern, and this is a community living in fear. Back to you in the studio.'

'Anyone know this Harris fellow?' asked Wayman, turning to look round the room.

'I do,' said one of the officers. 'I went on a residential course with him a few years ago. He'd just made DI with Greater Manchester Police.'

'And?'

'He's a difficult man to like. Ex-army. Hard bastard. Not very communicative. Likes his whisky.'

'He can't be all bad then,' said Wayman. 'I don't suppose you happen to remember which brand he drinks?'

'Actually, I do. Turns out we liked the same one. We shared a few belts.'

'Nip out and get me a bottle will you?'

'Guv?'

'If I were DCI Harris,' said Wayman, 'I'd be well pissed off if a bunch of hotshots from the city turned up on my doorstep, threatening to muscle in on my inquiry. We're going to need all the help we can get, I think.'

'Especially with Jack Harris. He's not the most welcoming person first time you meet him. It took me a day and a half to get him to even talk to me.'

'In which case,' said Wayman with a slight smile, 'make it two bottles, will you?'

Chapter nineteen

After taking the dogs for a walk round the corridors of the police station, diplomatically avoiding the commander's office, Jack Harris returned to his own room and sat down at his desk where weariness briefly overwhelmed him. He closed his eyes. The inspector felt a sudden need for sleep. He also felt a headache coming on and, reluctantly opening his eyes again, he reached into his desk for a packet of painkillers. He'd been fighting the temptation to take them for hours but the hangover caused by the three large whiskies he had thrown back when he got in at 2am was finally catching up with him.

Tablets taken, Harris stood up and walked over to the window where he stared wistfully across the roofs up at the hills, their tops now partially obscured by the wisps of cloud that were descending on the valley. The inspector sighed; the main reason for his return to Levton Bridge had been to reconnect with the high areas of the North Pennines. They represented something deep within him, something that had been lost to a life travelling the world with the army and during his years working in Manchester, but at times like this the inspector felt that the disconnection persisted.

Now, as always during the turbulence of major enquiries, he found himself craving the peace of the hills more than ever. Thought of connections drove him back to his desk as his mind turned to the investigation in hand and Gallagher's words *I just can't help feeling that we're missing something*. As he sat there, more words came to mind, this time drifting from the past. They were the words of his mentor when he joined CID at Greater Manchester Police. An experienced officer close to retirement, the detective had taken a keen interest in Harris's progression and had always said *Concentrate on what you know, not what you think you know*. Not for the first time, Harris gave a nod of thanks to his old friend and decided to peruse what he knew for certain.

The inspector took a piece of paper out of the top drawer and jotted down the name John Halstead, which he circled. He sat and stared at it for a few moments then drew a line to another circle for people who might wish Halstead harmed. The inspector scribbled the names Thomas Oldroyd, Lighting the Way, Jim Miles and Anne Gerrard. Then he drew another circle and wrote the name Dennis McGuffin, after which he created a line leading to a circle in which he wrote the names of the same people, before adding Henry Grace and Tony Gerrard. Harris shook his head and scored them both out. Gallagher was right; Henry Grace had no reason to murder McGuffin and, much as Tony Gerrard might worry that McGuffin might find out about his wife's links with Lighting the Way, it was asking too much to think him capable of murder.

When the inspector had finished the exercise, he sat back, surveyed his handiwork and pursed his lips. It had not taken him any further. If anything, it had only served to highlight the lack of progress in the case. *I just can't help feeling that we're missing something*. Inwardly cursing Gallagher for offering hope to Curtis, Harris threw his pen down onto the desk; it bounced off and clattered into the radiator, startling the dogs.

'Sorry, guys,' he said.

There was a light knock on the door and Matty Gallagher walked in.

'Shouldn't you be off to the Roxham Herald?' said the inspector grumpily, ignoring the sergeant's cheery demeanour.

'Yeah, I am, but I thought I'd do some checking before I went.' Gallagher pointed to the inspector's drawings. 'You been playing nice?'

Harris slid the piece of paper across the desk.

'You're right,' he said.

'It's a curse, I am afraid. But I manage to live with it. What am I right about this time?'

'We *are* missing something.' Harris walked across to retrieve his pen from Scoot, who had started to chew it. 'But I'm damned if I can work out what it is.'

'In which case, allow me to enlighten the way,' said Gallagher. He grinned. 'As it were.'

He waited for the inspector to place the pen back on the desk then picked it up, grimacing as he felt the dog's saliva on his hand. Having wiped it clean with his handkerchief, the sergeant leaned over the desk and wrote the name Tony Gerrard in a circle of its own. Harris watched in fascination as the sergeant then slowly and deliberately drew a line directly linking the two men.

'What's the connection?' asked the inspector. He gave him a quizzical look. 'Both journalists? It's a bit weak, isn't it?'

'Not just journalists,' said Gallagher. He took a seat. 'Journalists on the same paper – at the same time.'

'Really?'

'Yeah. Do you remember that Oldroyd said John Halstead started his career at the Roxham Herald before he moved onto The Derby Standard?'

Harris nodded.

'Well,' continued Gallagher, 'I've just come off the phone to a very pleasant woman in the HR Department at the Standard, and it's true. John Halstead *was* a journalist with them for four and a half years in the mid-Noughties. She's worked there for donkey's years and remembers him well. Even went out with him for a couple of months. Said he was a pleasant enough man if a bit secretive.'

'And Gerrard was there at the same time?'

'He was indeed. The Leicester Standard is part of the same group so I asked if he was ever at Derby with John Halstead and she said their times at the paper overlapped by about eighteen months. Gerrard and Halstead were reporters together. Gerrard lied when he said he did not know him.'

'Intriguing but…' Harris tapped the piece of paper, 'is it strong enough to suspect him of being a killer?'

'I always think lying is a good start.'

'Yeah, so do I. But where does Dennis McGuffin fit into the picture? It might mean Gerrard has some awkward questions to answer, might even put him in the frame for killing Halstead if there was some sort of falling out, but not McGuffin, surely?'

'Well, that's where you're wrong. See, Gerrard and Halstead did not just work together; they were also big drinking buddies as well. According to the HR woman, they even had a few couples nights together. Her and John Halstead with Tony Gerrard and his girlfriend.'

'Anne?'

'No, this was way before Anne. It was all very tragic – and of great interest to us.'

'Why tragic?'

'Gerrard's girlfriend was a nineteen-year-old called Elaine Murphy, a secretary at the Derby Standard, who was found murdered on a patch of wasteland close to the city centre in November 2006. Whoever did it used so much force that he could not get the knife out of her neck. Left her pinned to the ground.'

Harris sat forward in his chair.

'Interesting indeed,' he said, a gleam in his eyes. 'Go on.'

'Well, according to the HR woman, Gerrard was heartbroken at her death and transferred to work at the Leicester Standard not long afterwards. Couldn't bear to stay in Derby. Too many memories, he said. The HR woman bumped into him at some do a year later and said he was a shadow of his former self.'

'And Halstead?'

'Her relationship with him fizzled out not long after Elaine Murphy died. She said it wasn't going anywhere and always reckoned he was not open enough about himself.'

'The way he led his life, it would seem.'

'Indeed. Anyway, he left the paper not long afterwards and she lost contact with him. Had no idea where he was until I rang. Really shook her up, I can tell you.'

Harris sat back in his chair and nodded approvingly.

'Good work, good work indeed, Matty lad,' he said. 'Although I'm not quite sure where it takes us. Was anyone ever charged with the murder?'

'No, they weren't but according to the woman in HR, there's some sort of new investigation under way. Just started. A couple of Derby detectives came to talk to people at the office a few days ago, apparently. See if the passage of time had loosened any tongues.

'Cold case review?'

'I'm guessing so.' Gallagher picked up the inspector's pen again. 'What's more, the original investigation team did have one suspect that they were interested in.'

The sergeant slowly and deliberately underlined the name Dennis McGuffin. Harris stared at it for a few moments.

'You are kidding,' he said eventually.

'Nope.' Gallagher beamed. 'See, at the time, Dennis McGuffin was Circulation Manager at the Derby Standard. There had been rumours of a liaison between him and

Elaine Murphy for ages, although the HR woman reckons there was nothing to it. The original inquiry team seems to have agreed: they interviewed McGuffin but did not follow it up.'

'And were they right to do so, do you think?'

'They seem to have thought she was a hooker, so who knows? According to the HR woman, Halstead and Gerrard confronted McGuffin about it but he denied it. There was a real shouting match and, not long after, McGuffin was transferred to one of the group's papers in Bury. I checked, and he was there for seven years before retiring and moving to Levton Bridge with his wife.'

'And then he turns up nailed to a tree,' said Harris. He stood up. 'Time to see our Mr Gerrard, I think.'

'Don't you want to talk to the Derby detectives first?'

'Nope.'

'But…'

'If they want us, they'll find us.'

Gallagher shrugged.

'Your call,' he said.

'Always is,' said Harris, heading for the door.

They were in the corridor when the inspector's desk phone rang. Harris walked back into the room and picked up the receiver.

'Harris,' he said.

'I gather you want to talk to me,' said a gruff voice at the other end. 'How the Devil are you?'

'Devil's the word, Graham,' said Harris. The inspector sat down and cupped his hand over the receiver as Gallagher followed him back into the room. 'You get down there and hold on to him until I arrive. Take some back-up.'

Gallagher waved a hand and disappeared into the corridor.

* * *

151

The rain had started to fall from gloomy mid-afternoon skies when the car with DCI Grant Wayman in the front passenger seat and two of his detectives in the back swept out of the yard at the police station in Derby and emerged into the busy city centre traffic.

'How long will it take us to get to Levton Bridge?' asked Wayman, looking across at the driver.

'Three hours if we're lucky. Depends how bad the traffic is. It's all roadworks on the M6.' The driver glanced at the dashboard clock. 'I can't see us getting there much before six, six thirty.'

'Do the best you can,' said Wayman.

The DCI took his mobile phone out of his jacket pocket and dialled a number, pressing the button to put the call on speaker so that the others could hear the conversation.

'Levton Bridge Police,' said a woman's voice. 'How can I help you?'

'Can you put me through to DCI Harris, please?'

'I am afraid I have just put a call through to him. Who is it speaking, please?'

'This is DCI Grant Wayman from Derbyshire Police.'

'Does he know you?'

'What?'

'Does he know you?' repeated the Control Room operator.

'Er, no he doesn't. Look, this is very important. Any chance you can interrupt his call?'

'Not sure I can do that, sir,' said the operator. 'DCI Harris would not be very pleased. Would you like to leave a message instead?'

'Not really,' said Wayman. 'Does he have a mobile number I can ring?'

'I cannot give it out, I am afraid.'

'It really is very urgent,' said Wayman. He tried to keep the growing frustration out of his voice. 'I really do need to talk to him as soon as possible.'

'I am sorry but DCI Harris is most insistent that we do not give out his mobile number. Like I say, I can take a message, though.'

'And will he ring back?' asked Wayman.

The woman hesitated.

'Oh, I'm sure he will,' she said eventually. She did not sound certain. 'But he is very busy at the moment. Do you want to give me your name and number then?'

'No, it's alright,' said Wayman curtly, 'I'll try again later.'

'As you wish,' said the operator and the line went dead.

'Fucking hell,' said Wayman. He turned round to look at the officers in the back seat and shook his head in disbelief. 'What kind of a bloody operation do they run up there?'

'I told you,' said the other officer. 'He's an awkward customer is Jack Harris. Very awkward indeed.'

'So it would seem,' said Wayman. He glanced at the driver. 'Step on it, Bri. Jack Harris is going to need our help whether he likes it or not.'

Chapter twenty

Once Gallagher had left Harris's office to find a couple of uniformed officers to accompany him to Roxham, the inspector returned to his phone call.

'Sorry, Graham,' he said into the receiver. 'Things are a bit manic here.'

'I can imagine,' said Leckie. 'You got yourself a suspect then?'

Harris tipped back in his seat and put his feet up on the desk, teetering precariously for a second or two before securing his balance.

'I didn't until five minutes ago,' he said. 'Looks like I might have now, though, but I could still do with some help.'

'Don't tell me, yokel bobbies struggling to turn their steam computer on again?'

'Something like that.'

Graham Leckie was one of the few people who could get away with a talking to Jack Harris in that way. A uniformed constable with Greater Manchester Police, Leckie was one of the inspector's closest friends, the two having met some years previously when Harris worked for the force. Initially, they had connected through their shared love of wildlife but after Harris moved north to Levton Bridge, they still talked regularly because Graham Leckie worked in force intelligence and the valley regularly witnessed crimes committed by criminals from further south.

'Who's your suspect then?' asked Leckie. 'You allowed to tell me?'

'Actually, we're looking at a local newspaper editor. There may be a link between him, our killings and a murder in Derby a few years ago.'

'A journalist, eh? That'll please you.' Leckie gave a low chuckle. 'You'd lock them all up if you could. Where do I come into it then? Your editor a Manchester lad?'

'No, I need help on another possibility. That our murders could be linked to a religious group that settled in our area a few weeks ago.'

'And you thought of the holiest person you knew?'

'Not quite, Graham. Wondered if I could run a name past you?'

'Fire away.'

'John Halstead. He's one of the victims.'

'He the guy on the allotment?' asked Leckie; Harris could hear him tapping on his keyboard.

'That's him.'

'I had an allotment for ten years and I tell you this, Hawk. there's more to these gardening types than meets the eye. You want me to check if we've got anyone on record for armed shrubbery?'

'You and Matty Gallagher should form a comedy double act,' said Harris, but he was smiling. 'Or go on Gardeners' Question Time.'

'Thought you'd appreciate it. Why should we know about this Halstead fellow then?'

'We think he has a link with a GMP inquiry a few years ago. A couple and their daughter who kept some young girls locked up for years.'

'I remember it well. A bloke with a straggly beard who thought he was God but turned out to be a retired binman from Oldham. There's a joke in there somewhere. Yup, Halstead's here. Looks like he was some form of private investigator who sold the story to a newspaper.'

'Then helped CID?'

'Looks like it.' Leckie typed again. 'Our lot contacted him after the story appeared in the paper and slipped him a few quid for what he knew. His name never came out because the cult leaders pleaded guilty. Hang on, this is weird, though. Someone's put a note on here saying that Halstead died in a car crash in Leicestershire earlier this year.'

'Well, *someone* did.'

'You've got a strange one there, me old son.'

'Tell me about it.' There was a knock on the door and Harris looked up to see Butterfield. He gestured for her to come in. 'Got to go, Graham, let me know if you dig up anything else, will you? Oh, can you do me another quick check first? You ever investigated a bloke called Dennis McGuffin? He worked for a newspaper in Bury. Circulation Manager.'

'You and your newspaper folk.' More tapping. 'Sorry, nothing. Listen, before you go, we keep promising ourselves that walk to check out the peregrine nest site at Holkham Crag. Want to sort something when you've finished your murder inquiry?'

'Sounds good. Haven't been to check it for ages and the dogs will appreciate the walk. Talk later.' Harris replaced the receiver, lowered his feet to the floor and looked at Butterfield. 'You look like you've got some news to impart, Constable.'

'Motorway Police have just picked up David Fulton and the others in a service station near Preston.'

'They didn't get far.'

'Apparently, they've driven in circles waiting for God to tell them which direction to go in.'

'And did he?'

'Apparently not. They ran out of diesel and didn't have the money to buy any more, and their credit card was blocked.'

Harris gave a low laugh.

'They're bringing them back up here in a car,' said Butterfield. 'They say they'll bring the minibus as well but they're going to put it on a recovery truck so it'll be a while. Oh, and Stella Gaunt from Leicestershire is here. She's in the squad room.'

'Excellent.'

Butterfield hesitated.

'Is there something else?' asked Harris. He gestured for the constable to sit down. 'What's eating you?'

She sat down and looked at him unhappily.

'I'm not sure I have handled things as well as I could have done, sir,' she said.

'I think a number of us could say that,' replied Harris, thinking about Henry Grace's complaint. 'What's your problem?'

'The way I talked to the DI. I know that I can sometimes come over as a bit pushy but I think that I overdid it this time.'

'Long may it continue, Constable.

'Sir?'

'The day a police officer stops standing up for what they believe is right, is the day to hand in the badge.' The inspector gave her a reassuring look. 'Pushy or not.'

'But the DI…'

'Don't you worry about the DI,' said Harris. He stood up. 'She's more pissed off with herself that she didn't take Lighting the Way more seriously than worrying about you. Come one, let's go and see Stella. Welcome her to Levton Bridge.'

Before the inspector could get out of the room, his desk phone rang. Harris picked up the receiver.

'Graham, that was quick,' he said.

'I'm not Graham,' said a voice he had never heard; the inspector could hear that the man was talking from a fast-moving car. 'Am I talking to DCI Jack Harris, by any chance?'

'You are. And you would be?'

'DCI Grant Wayman, Derbyshire Police. You're a difficult man to get hold of. Very difficult indeed.'

Harris waved a hand at Butterfield.

'I'll see you there,' he said.

Once the constable had left the room, the inspector returned his attention to the caller.

'Yeah, I'm sorry about that,' said Harris. The inspector gave a slight smile. He sensed how this was going to go. 'Been a bit busy today. How can I help you?'

'You and I appear to working different ends of the same inquiry, I think. Elaine Murphy.'

'So I believe.'

'And were you going to ring me at any point?' There was an edge to Wayman's voice now. 'I don't know how you do things up there, but in Derby, we make sure that…'

'I've only just found out myself.' Harris decided not to rise to the bait; there would be time enough for that. He liked the idea of tussling with a new adversary. 'Besides, I *was* going to ring you once we'd picked Tony Gerrard up.'

'Picked him up?' said Wayman. 'Picked him up why?'

'He's a suspect in our double murder. You interested in him as well?'

'Very much so.'

'You suspect him of killing Elaine?'

'No.'

'Then why so interested?'

'He's a witness. So was Halstead. They may know the identity of the murderer.'

'Dennis McGuffin?'

'You know about that then?' Wayman was surprised to find himself intimidated by the staccato barrage of questions and thrown by the inspector's knowledge of the case. 'Look, are you formally arresting Gerrard?'

'My sergeant is doing that now, yes.'

'Well, I'd like to talk to him as well,' said Wayman.

'Happy for you to do that once we've finished with him.'

'I'd rather do it at the same time. It's in both our interests. We'll be with you in less than two hours.'

'You're already on your way?' It was Harris's turn to be wrong-footed.

'Yeah, we're on the motorway.'

'No need to break the speed limit. It'll be a while before we've finished with him.'

'I take it you are not minded to let us sit in on the interview then?'

'I'm not so sure that's a good idea, Grant. Besides, suspect trumps witness in my book. As does the fact that you'll be in my town.'

'Well, the procedure in Derby…'

'You won't be in Derby,' said Harris. 'Worth remembering that. Anyway, we'll sort it when you arrive. Got to go, an officer from Leicester CID has just got here.'

'Leicester CID? Why is…?'

'Just ask for me at the desk.'

And with a smile, Harris put the phone down.

'City boys,' he said, then stood up and headed out of the office, dogs trotting obediently at his heels.

Grant Wayman heard the click as the line went dead. He stared out of the car window with a thunderous expression on his face.

'Fucking yokels,' he growled.

'Jack Harris may be many things,' said the detective who knew the inspector, 'but yokel he isn't. I tell you, the man is one prickly customer.'

'Well if it's a fight he wants, it's a fight he's going to get,' said Wayman. 'Even if I have to bang his fucking head off the wall.'

'I'm not so sure that would be such a good idea. He looks like he can handle himself and you...'

The detective did not finish the sentence as a fierce glare from Wayman silenced him. And no one reminded the DCI about his comments on respect.

* * *

A few moments after finishing his conversation with Grant Wayman, Harris strode into the CID room to be met by Butterfield and a slim short-haired blonde woman in her late twenties.

'Stella,' he said politely. He extended a hand in greeting. 'How nice to see you again.'

He remembered her now.

Chapter twenty-one

Tony Gerrard knew that they'd come for him the moment Gallagher and the two uniformed officers walked into the newsroom and he saw the grim expression on their faces. The officers spotted him standing by the door to his office and walked towards him, watched in stunned silence by the other journalists. Gerrard was not surprised that the police were there, he had known that they would work it out eventually, he just did not think they would make the connection this quickly. He gestured for them to follow him into the office where he closed the door and sat down behind his desk. He decided to play it cool.

'I assume this is not a social visit?' he said.

'I am afraid not,' said the sergeant. 'We are here to arrest you on suspicion of involvement in the murders of Dennis McGuffin and John Halstead.'

'My turn, is it?'

'What?'

'I must be the only person in the valley you have not arrested. You've got Thomas Oldroyd, some bloke from the allotments and Anne told me that you've even kept Jim Miles in for questioning as well. Why on earth would you think that the vicar was involved, for pity's sake?'

'Because he, like you, has been keeping secrets.' Gallagher could not conceal his irritation at the editor's attitude. Lack of sleep was catching up with the sergeant and he was in no mood for games. 'And there's nothing that a detective dislikes more than secrets.'

'I don't know what you are…'

'Time to cut the act, Mr Gerrard,' said Gallagher. 'We know about Elaine Murphy. You must have known that we would find out sooner or later, yet you still kept it from us.'

The mention of the dead woman's name seemed to have a profound effect on the editor. Within seconds, his eyes were glistening with tears. Gallagher watched him; the sergeant was always fascinated by the way people changed when presented with difficult truths.

'Why did you not tell us?' asked the detective.

'I did not mention her,' said Gerrard quietly, 'because she has nothing to do with what has happened in Levton Bridge. How did you find out?'

'I don't really think we should talk about it until you are being formally interviewed,' said the sergeant. 'To your feet, please.'

'Are you not going to answer my…?'

'To your feet!'

'You are about to lead me through my own newsroom in handcuffs, in front of my staff,' said the editor. He was struggling to form words as the emotion threatened to overwhelm him. 'I think that you owe me some form of explanation.'

Gallagher thought for a moment, his flash of irritation dissipating as quickly as it had arrived as he looked at the journalist's distressed expression.

'I guess it can't do any harm,' he said. 'The police in Derby have re-opened the investigation into her death. A cold case review.'

'And not before time. Perhaps they'll do it right this time. Did they ask you to arrest me then?'

'No, we found out from the HR woman at the Standard. She said that Dennis McGuffin knew you and John Halstead when you worked there.'

'Ah, dear Cynthia,' said Gerrard with a smile. 'She always did like to gossip. If Derby Police have not contacted you, do I take it you are here because you have worked out that I, above just about anyone else, had good reason to kill Dennis McGuffin?'

'You certainly had motive.'

'Well, I didn't kill him but, I'll tell you now, Sergeant, I'm glad that someone did and I hope that whoever it was made the bastard suffer as much as he did Elaine.'

'So, it's true that you suspect Dennis killed her?'

'Not suspect. *Know*. She rebuffed his advances, and he stabbed her then left her to die among the detritus of people's lives on that wasteland. Wicked. Wicked.'

'Except the police at the time did not think that he was responsible for her death.'

'Them!' The comment was spat out. 'They didn't want to know. They'd already made up their mind that, because Elaine's body was found in an area used by hookers, she must have been a street girl who was killed by a punter.'

'And she wasn't?'

'She was as sweet a girl as you could ever imagine was Elaine,' he said, his voice much quieter, the anger gone. Tears started in his eyes. 'And as devout as they come. Went to church every Sunday. Sometimes twice, morning and evening.'

'Was she part of Lighting the Way?'

'No, it was before them. Besides, she would not have had anything to do with a bunch of cranks like that. A very conventional girl was Elaine and she did not deserve to die the way she did. I tell you, it was Dennis McGuffin who killed her. He denied it, of course. The man was a letch and always tried to bluster his way out of it, but I knew. Me and John, we both knew. John always said that you could see it in his eyes.'

Gerrard stood up and held out his arms.

'Go on then,' he said. 'Put the cuffs on. Let's get this over with.'

Gallagher looked at him for a few moments, saw how the tears were streaming down the journalist's face and shook his head.

'I don't think that will be necessary,' he said. 'Somehow I don't think you're going to make a run for it.'

'Thank you,' said the editor. 'Thank you.'

* * *

'Like I told Chief Inspector Harris here,' said Thomas Oldroyd, looking across the interview room desk at Stella Gaunt, 'I will admit to assaulting John Halstead in Ravensdale Road but nothing else.'

'It's more complicated than that,' said the Leicestershire detective. 'We believe that John Halstead staged his own death and we want to know why – and who really died in the car crash.'

'I know nothing about that.' Oldroyd looked at Harris. 'Or about your murders, Chief Inspector. And you have nothing that says otherwise, do you?'

Harris did not reply but both men knew it was true. Oldroyd looked back at Stella Gaunt.

'Are you going to charge me then?' he asked.

'It was a very minor offence, Thomas,' she said.

'Not to me, it isn't. I have lived with the guilt for six months.'

'To be honest, I'm more interested in the body in the car.'

'And I told you that I know nothing about it,' said Oldroyd. He stood up. 'Unless you want to explain to your boss why you wasted time and money travelling up here, you had better charge me or I walk out of here right now.'

'Sit down,' growled Harris.

Oldroyd hesitated for a few moments then did as he was told.

'It's like you want to be charged, Thomas,' said Gaunt. 'Why would you want that, Thomas? I don't understand.'

'It would represent absolution for my sin.'

Gaunt looked at Harris, who shrugged.

'Don't ask me,' said the inspector. 'It's out of my area of expertise. As Thomas reminded me a couple of hours ago, I'm not a priest.'

'OK,' said the Leicestershire officer. 'I'll charge you with assault.'

Oldroyd gave a sigh of relief.

'Thank you,' he said. 'I feel like a weight has been lifted from my mind.'

'That's the first time anyone has ever said that when I've told them they were going to be charged,' replied Stella Gaunt.

* * *

Twenty minutes later, with Oldroyd charged and in a cell, Harris and Gaunt repaired to the inspector's office where they were greeted by an excited Scoot and Archie.

'You're allowed to bring them to work?' said Gaunt as she ruffled Archie's head.

'No,' said Harris. He moved over to the kettle. 'Tea?'

Gaunt sat down.

'Please,' she said. 'What should I do with Thomas Oldroyd then? I don't particularly want to take him back down to Leicester with me.'

'His car's here anyway,' said Harris. 'Sitting in the yard.'

'And you're not holding him for the murders?'

Harris turned round, tea caddy in hand.

'Nope,' he said. 'Forensics have found very little of use at either site and his car's clean. Basically, we have found nothing to connect him with either of the killings and no evidence that he has an accomplice. I'd cut him loose, if I were you. I think he's telling the truth when he

165

says that he knows nothing about the body in the car. If you ask me, the answer died on that allotment last night.'

Gaunt sighed.

'I'm afraid you may be right,' she said. 'And Thomas is right as well. My governor won't be happy. He's stressed enough about the budgets as it is and the hotel is setting me back a hundred and thirty quid.'

'You're staying overnight?' Harris returned to his tea-making and tried not to sound too interested.

'Thought I'd be here longer.'

'You could cancel it. Go back tonight.'

'It's a long drive, and our Chief Constable is big on officers not driving when they're tired. There have been one or two near misses.'

'Good for him,' said Harris. 'Where you staying?'

'The Manor Hotel. Off the marketplace. You know it?'

'Nice place.'

There was a knock on the door, and a uniformed officer walked in.

'Jack,' he said, 'there's a DCI Wayman at the front counter asking to see you. Says you know what it's about. Oh, and the religious cranks have turned up. What do you want me to do with them?'

'Ask the DI to talk to them. Oh, and ask forensics to take a look at their minibus when it turns up, will you? The cops down there are putting it on a recovery truck.'

'Will do. And DCI Wayman? He was most insistent.'

'I'll bet he was. You can send him up.'

The uniformed officer glanced at Stella Gaunt, gave the merest of smiles and walked back into the corridor.

'Not Grant Wayman?' said Gaunt, when the officer had gone. 'From Derby?'

'Yeah, he's interested in the fact that we have lifted the journalist who wrote the piece about the incident at Ravensdale Road.'

'Tony Gerrard? Why have you done that?'

'He works in the town at the bottom of the valley now and it turns out there'sa link with the death of a teenage girl in Derby a few years back. Wayman has re-opened the case. You know him then?'

'Unfortunately.'

'Why unfortunately?'

'I was seconded to Derby for six months when I first became a detective. My boss thought it would be character-building. Wayman was the DI at the time.'

'And you weren't impressed?'

'The man's a misogynist. It was the worst six months of my career. I spent most of the time doing his paperwork and making his coffee. I was so relieved to get back to Leicester. What's the murder he's re-investigating? Not Elaine Murphy, by any chance?'

'Yeah, you know about it?'

'Wayman was a DC on the case. It's the only murder he ever worked on that wasn't solved. It's kind of personal with him, I think.' She stood up. 'Look, I don't particularly want to see him again, Jack. Are you OK if I release Oldroyd then make myself scarce?'

'Sure.'

'I'll be at the hotel if you need me.' She stood up and gave a slight smile. 'Thanks for the offer of a cup of tea. Maybe some other time, eh?'

'Maybe,' said Harris.

And then she was gone, leaving the distracted inspector to wonder if he was reading too much into the smile while trying to focus on what he was going to say to his visitor. He decided to be firm but not aggressive; the last thing he wanted was Wayman making a complaint to Curtis. The relationship between Harris and the commander may have continued to improve but the inspector knew that he still had to be careful, especially with two high profile murders on his hands. A couple of minutes later, Grant Wayman walked into the inspector's office, clutching a black hold-all bag.

'Jack Harris?' he said.

'The very same.'

'Grant Wayman.'

'I guessed.'

'It's good to meet you,' said Wayman, hoping it came over as sincere.

The detectives reached across the desk and shook hands, each noting the firmness of the other's grip. Harris gestured for Wayman to take a seat and sat down behind his desk. After they had surveyed each other for a few moments, big beasts sizing each other up before entering the fray, the Derby detective surprised his counterpart by reaching down into his bag and producing a bottle of whisky which he placed on the table and slid towards Harris.

'I think we got off on the wrong tack earlier,' he said. 'This is your favourite, I believe.'

'You seem remarkably well-informed.'

'One of my team met you on a course a few years back. When you were with Greater Manchester. Says you like your whisky.'

'I'm still not going to let you sit in on our interview with Tony Gerrard,' replied Harris.

'Yeah, I thought you'd say that.' Wayman reached down and produced a second bottle which he placed next to the first.

'On the other hand,' said Harris.

* * *

Thomas Oldroyd stepped out into the darkening light of the afternoon and stood in the police yard, savouring the fresh air for a few moments. The uniformed officer next to him passed over Oldroyd's car keys and headed back into the building.

Oldroyd took his mobile out of his coat pocket and dialled a number.

'Charlie,' he said. 'Where are you?'

'Roxham,' said Charles Daniels. 'I've booked into that B &B on Lowton Street. I'm keeping my head down, like we agreed.

'I'll come and get you,' said Oldroyd, unlocking the car door. 'We've got work to do.'

Chapter twenty-two

Detective Inspector Gillian Roberts sat and looked across the desk at the long-haired young man with the silver crucifix hanging round his neck. Neil Harker, for his part, looked bewildered. Something about him reminded Roberts of her eldest son; a vulnerability, a sense that the world was so big and he so small. The detective was undergoing conflict of her own; the revelation that JohnHalstead thought that Lighting the Way was akin to a cult had caused her to question everything she had heard about them. Wonder if Edie Prentice and the others were right. Wonder yet again if she had made a mistake.

As usual when faced with moral dilemmas, the police officer within Gillian Roberts won out. Lighting the Way, she decided, had too many questions to answer for there not to be something amiss. The inspector thought of her son, glanced at Gallagher, who was sitting next to her, then reached out to gently touch Neil Harker's hand.

'You're safe now, lovey,' she said.

'I don't feel safe.' Harker withdrew his hand and gave her a bemused look.

'I know, lovey, but no one can hurt you now. You're free of their hold.'

Harker looked surprised.

'Hold,' he said. 'What do you mean?'

'We know that John Halstead thought you were being held against your will by the Fultons,' said Gallagher. 'You and your girlfriend. Jacqueline, isn't it?'

'We're not being held against our will,' said Harker. 'Why on earth would you think that? We want to be part of Lighting the Way.'

'Yes, but…'

'You don't understand, do you,' said Harker. 'None of you understand. You're persecuting us.'

'OK then, so what don't we understand?'

'For a start, you don't understand what Lighting the Way means to us. Before they found me, I was lost. I'd tried to kill myself twice. I couldn't see any future. Then I met Jacqueline and she introduced me to the others, and everything changed. Lighting the Way offers us something beautiful. A reason to live.'

Roberts considered the comment for a few moments; something about the earnestness of his look, the way his eyes shone when he spoke, confirmed to her that Neil Harker was telling the truth. That he and the others were innocent.

'Everyone needs something to hold onto,' said Harker.

'I suspect they do, lovey,' said Roberts eventually. 'I suspect they do.'

Matty Gallagher said nothing.

* * *

In another part of Levton Bridge Police Station, Jack Harris and Grant Wayman sat and looked across the desk at Tony Gerrard, who was perspiring profusely in the hot little interview room. Any previous pretence at calmness had gone; Gerrard was a man hemmed in by his situation and frightened of the consequences. Both detectives sensed that if he was given a little push, he would reveal what he knew.

'So,' said Harris, 'let's go through it again, shall we, Tony? We think that you may be responsible for the death of Dennis McGuffin and possibly also John Halstead…'

'And I've told you I'm not. How many times? John Halstead was a friend and, as for Dennis McGuffin, I may have detested the sleazeball, but there's no way I would have killed him.'

'But you had motive,' said Harris.

'Motive to hate not to kill. There's a difference, Chief Inspector. You have nothing to prove that I killed him.'

Harris looked at Wayman.

'Are you going to tell him or shall I?' said Harris.

'I think I should,' said Wayman.

'Tell me what?' Gerrard looked anxious.

'Why do you think Dennis McGuffin killed Elaine?' asked Wayman, ignoring the editor's question.

'I told you, he'd been pestering her to sleep with him for ages, would not take no for an answer. I think she rejected him one time too many and he killed her for it. But why do you care? You think she was a hooker. I despaired when I heard that the new inquiry team still thought that …'

'Hang on,' said Harris. He looked at Wayman. 'I thought you said you had not talked to him about the new investigation?'

'We haven't. It was on our to-do list. In fact, this is the first time I have ever met Mr Gerrard. The original interview with him just after the murder was done by my governor.'

'Then how,' asked Harris, staring hard at the editor, 'did you know that the new investigation was not focusing on McGuffin?'

Gerrard shifted in his seat.

'I just guessed,' he said.

'Try again,' said Harris.

Gerrard hesitated.

'For fuck's sake,' exclaimed Harris. 'Will you just tell us the truth? I'm sick of people lying.'

'OK,' said Gerrard reluctantly. 'I knew because Cynthia rang me. She said that the police had been to see people at the Standard and were still talking as if they thought Elaine was a hooker. Cynthia tried to tell them about Dennis McGuffin but they would not listen.'

Gerrard glared at Wayman.

'*You* would not listen,' he said, pointing a finger at him. 'McGuffin said he was at home alone when Elaine was killed. No one to corroborate it and yet you still would not consider him a suspect. Me and John tried to tell your DCI at the time but he just wouldn't have it.'

'I admit that we did not take him seriously enough,' said Wayman, 'but what you will not know, what no one knows, is that we have carried out new DNA tests on Elaine's clothing and when the results came back yesterday they revealed a link to someone else.'

Gerrard stared at him in disbelief.

'Not McGuffin?' he said in a quiet voice.

'I am afraid not. The DNA suggests that it was one of the newspaper's delivery drivers. That's why we planned to interview you, see if you knew anything about him and where he might be now. He seems to have dropped out of sight.'

Gerrard stared at the DCI, apparently struggling to comprehend what he was being told.

'So Dennis McGuffin did not kill her?' he said eventually.

'We think it was a man called Frank Archer. The DNA suggests that he may have been responsible for a couple of unsolved rapes as well.'

'Oh, God,' groaned Gerrard. He buried his face in his hands. 'What have I done?'

'Just what we were wondering,' said Harris, leaning forward. 'What have you done?'

* * *

'You've got it all wrong,' said David Fulton. He looked earnestly across the interview room table at Roberts and Gallagher. 'Neil and Jacqueline were never our prisoners. Far from it.'

'You can see why we might have thought that to be the case, though,' said the sergeant. 'You were not exactly open about things last night, were you, David? You couldn't get rid of us quickly enough – and you *did* do a moonlit flit.'

'I know it must have seemed like I was hiding something when you came to see us but it's only because I am trying to protect Neil and Jacqueline.'

'Protect them from what?'

'From the outside world, especially after what happened in Leicester. They are very fragile souls, and we offer them refuge. The last thing I wanted was for you to scare them.'

'Let's say we believe you,' said the detective inspector before Gallagher could reply. 'Why would John Halstead think that they were being held against their will?'

'I'm not sure that he did. I just think he wanted to make some quick money. I believe he thought the police would buy information off him, no questions asked, after the success he had with that cult in Oldham.'

'So, you knew what he was doing?' asked Gallagher.

'It took a while to believe what Thomas was telling us but eventually, yes.'

'And you did what?'

'We said we would forgive him and let him stay with us, but Thomas disagreed. He said that John had tried to destroy Lighting the Way and could not be trusted. Everything blew apart, and we did not see either of them after the incident in the pub. Thomas sent a few unpleasant texts but that was all. I'm sure it was all just words, though. He wouldn't ever harm us. Then we heard John had died in a road accident.'

'Did you know that he was still alive?' asked Gallagher.

'Not until he turned up at the farm a few days ago. It was a shock, I can tell you.'

'Why did he come to see you?' asked Roberts.

'He said he wanted to rejoin Lighting the Way. That he regretted what he had done.'

'And what did you say?'

'That we would take him back.'

'Even after what he did?' said Gallagher, the disbelief clear in his voice. 'What happened to protecting Neil and Jacqueline from the big, bad world?'

'I don't expect you to understand, Sergeant, but no door is ever closed in the House of the Lord and we believe in the power of repentance.'

'And did he re-join you?' asked Roberts.

'He was going to. He said he had a couple of things to attend to in Leicester but that he would return.' Fulton looked sadly at the detectives. 'We never saw him again. Now we know why. Perhaps it was for the best. It might have been difficult if Thomas had agreed to rejoin as well…'

'Thomas Oldroyd?' said Gallagher sharply. 'When did you see him?'

'Last night. Him and another man we did not know. They came to the farm.'

'Why on earth did you not tell us this last night?' The sergeant's voice betrayed his intense frustration. 'You must have recognised the picture of John, and you knew that he and Thomas had a history of bad feeling.'

'Yes, but I am sure that it was nothing to do with the murder. Thomas was seeking absolution, remember.'

'Pha!' snorted Gallagher. 'You're off your fucking rockers, the lot of you!'

'Is that why he came to see you?' asked Roberts. She shot the sergeant a warning look to keep silent. 'To seek absolution?'

175

'Yes, but we cannot offer it. Only the Lord can do that. We offered to pray with him, but it wasn't enough.' Fulton sighed. 'If I'm honest, nothing was ever enough for Thomas. We are very different people but surely you do not think that he could be capable of murder?'

'It's possible,' said Roberts. 'And looking ever more possible the more we find out. Tell me, in what way are you different?'

Fulton hesitated. He seemed to be struggling with the words.

'In the kind of God we believe in,' he said eventually.

'And what kind of God is that?' asked Roberts. She felt a sick feeling in the pit of her stomach; she feared that she already knew the answer.

'We believe in the loving New Testament God but Thomas, I am afraid his parents were very devout and very strict and they taught him as a child to believe completely in the God of the Old Testament.'

'What's the difference?' asked Gallagher. He looked at the detective inspector. 'I mean, isn't it all the same bloke with a big white beard sitting in the clouds?'

'Not quite,' said Roberts quietly. 'You see, the Old Testament God is the God of vengeance.'

'And Thomas Oldroyd believes in that one hundred per cent,' said Fulton. 'And when his demons hold sway, he can be a frightening man.'

'And one who we have just released,' said Gallagher urgently. He stood up and headed for the door.

'There's something else I have not told you,' said Fulton.

'I hate to ask,' said Gallagher, turning back to him.

'John rang us up late yesterday afternoon. Said that he was in Levton Bridge on his way to see us. He sounded scared.'

'Of what?' asked the sergeant.

'He said that he had seen Thomas and a man he did not know drinking in a café in the town centre. He was not sure if they saw him.' Fulton's voice tailed off. 'We never heard from him again.'

'I think we can guess why,' said Gallagher and walked out into the corridor.

'Why did you not mention this earlier?' asked Roberts when the sergeant had gone,

'I knew it would look bad for Thomas,' said Fulton. 'I had faith that he was innocent.'

'Sometimes,' said Roberts, looking at him sadly, 'faith is not enough, David. I think you are going to have to learn that.'

* * *

'So what *have* you done, Tony?' asked Harris. 'Are you involved in the death of Dennis McGuffin?'

'I am afraid I might be,' said the editor with a heavy sigh. 'Although I did not want any of this to happen. You must believe me.'

'What do you mean?'

'Look, I admit that when I heard that the police were not looking at Dennis McGuffin for Elaine's murder, I was furious. I loved that woman. Absolutely adored her. It seemed so wrong that he should get away with it.'

'When did you realise that he had come to live in Levton Bridge?' asked Harris.

'A few weeks ago. The church put out a press release about some event, and he was quoted. It wasn't difficult to find out that it was the same man.'

'So, you confronted him?' said Harris.

'No, I tried to tell myself that it was all in the past and tried to ignore him but it kept gnawing away at me. The thought that he was still alive and Elaine was dead was too much to bear. Then I heard that the police were still not taking him seriously as a suspect and it all came flooding back.'

'And you did what?' asked Harris.

177

'I rang Thomas Oldroyd. I had his number from the texts he had sent to Anne.'

'Why ring him?' asked Wayman. He looked at Harris. 'From what I've heard, the guy's a bit of a screwball.'

'I thought he might still be in touch with the others. David Fulton is not exactly the most receptive of men and he hates journalists anyway, and I did not want to drag Anne into it.'

'Nice to hear that you still think of her occasionally,' said Harris. He decided not to mention the affair with the vicar.

'That's a low blow, Chief Inspector,' protested Gerrard. 'Just because I cared for Elaine does not mean I do not love my wife. Anyway, I thought if I told Thomas about McGuffin it might help them in their negotiations with the people at St Cuthbert's. Give them a bit of leverage.'

'I thought you hated Lighting the Way,' said Harris. 'Why on earth would you help them?'

'Yes, but I hated Dennis McGuffin more. I thought it might humiliate him, destroy his reputation, when the truth came out. Anyway, you can think what you want; I'm only telling you this to counteract whatever wild claims Thomas made to you when you interviewed him.'

'He didn't mention you,' said Harris.

'He didn't?'

'No.'

Gerrard thought for a few moments.

'In which case,' he said. 'I wish to say nothing more.'

There was a knock on the door, and Gallagher stepped into the room.

'Can I have a word?' he said, looking at Harris. 'It's urgent.'

The inspector was only out of the room for a couple of minutes. When he returned, Gerrard took one look at the grim expression on the detective's face and said: 'Look, I never meant for any of this to happen.'

'Ah, but I think you did,' said Harris. He sat down. 'I think you know what Thomas is like.'

'I have no idea what you are talking about.'

'You can drop the act,' snapped Harris. 'I think you know that if you push Thomas hard enough, he'll do anything to defend Lighting the Way.'

'That's rubbish!' said the editor.

'Is it? Is it really? You thought that if you told Thomas that McGuffin was making life difficult for David Fulton and the others at St Cuthbert's it might tip him over the edge. Especially if you happened to mention what you thought he'd done to a nice God-fearing woman like Elaine Murphy.'

'Jesus, you might as well have put a loaded gun in his hand,' said Wayman. 'It's like you killed him yourself.'

'Ah, but that's the point, isn't it?' said Gerrard. There was a wicked glint in his eye; a more calculating man had emerged. 'I didn't kill him, did I? So I told Thomas about McGuffin, so what? I didn't tell him to kill him. Or John Halstead, for that matter.'

'Yes, and what beef did you have with him?' asked Harris.

'None at all. He was a friend. I didn't even know that John was still alive. If Thomas killed him, they must have met by accident but it's nothing to do with me. You'll get nothing to stick in court.'

'Tell it to the judge,' said Harris.

'If it ever gets that far,' replied Gerrard and he sat back in his chair with a self-satisfied look on his face.

Chapter twenty-three

'Any word on Oldroyd?' asked Harris, looking up from his paperwork as Matty Gallagher walked into his office shortly after 8pm.

The sergeant slumped wearily into a chair and closed his eyes.

'A couple of possible sightings of the car,' he said. 'Nothing definite, though. Everyone's out looking for him. He'll not get far. However, we may have a lead on his accomplice.'

'Go on.'

'I managed to track down the father.' Gallagher opened his eyes. 'Thomas is right about his old man; he is a pompous so-and-so.'

'That's barristers for you.'

'Indeed it is. Anyway, like Thomas said, they hadn't talked for years, and it was clear from my conversation that the father didn't care what happened to his son. However, he did give me the name of the mental health unit in Wakefield where Oldroyd was held when he was a teenager. I rang them, and one of the staff told me that he used to be close to another patient called Charlie Daniels.'

'Who he?'

'An impressionable type, by all accounts. Very suggestible and with a penchant for setting fire to things. Wheelie bins, bus shelters and the like.'

'Why do we think it's him?' asked Harris.

'Charlie had been living at home since he lost his job as a swimming pool attendant a few weeks ago – set fire to paper towels in the changing rooms – but his mother reported him missing three days ago after Oldroyd got in touch with him.'

'Did you ring her?'

'Alison did. Mum said that Charlie had been behaving oddly, doing a mean and moody act ever since he left his job, but he cheered up after Thomas Oldroyd appeared on the doorstep. She knows Thomas from the health unit days and warned her son off; she knows how easily led her son is. They had a huge row and Charlie went missing. She has not heard from him since.'

'Local cops have anything on him?'

'What do you think?' said Gallagher. 'Missing person thirty-eight as far as they were concerned.'

'And now he could be a murderer.' Harris frowned. 'You know, Matty lad, it strikes me that a lot of people seem to have slipped through the cracks on this one.'

'They have. Oh, before I forget, we've just heard from Henry Grace,'

'As if we didn't have enough problems.'

'Oddly enough, he was more conciliatory. He's called an emergency meeting at the church.' Gallagher glanced at the wall clock. 'Starts in twenty minutes. Henry wondered if you would release the vicar so that he can attend? Apparently, they have some questions for him.'

'I imagine they have,' said Harris. 'OK, let's kick the lying bastard out. The Bishop's been onto Curtis three times already, demanding to know what's happening.'

* * *

181

Darkness was falling under gloomy late summer evening skies as the grim-faced parishioners arrived at St Cuthbert's for their crisis meeting, each one pushing their way through the heavy timber doors and filing in silence down the aisles to the two large tables set out at the far end of the church. The air was sharp and chill in the church and each person took their seat without speaking, not catching each other's eye, their expressions solemn, their faces partly obscured by the shadows cast by the candles lit on the altar.

Elsewhere in the church, the Reverend Jim Miles walked into the office to be greeted by Anne Gerrard, who flung her arms round him, tears starting in her eyes.

'You can't know how glad I am to see you,' she said, hugging him tightly. 'When did they release you?'

'Just now. Jack Harris gave me another of his lectures about lying then told me to get out of his sight.'

'Are they going to charge you?'

'I don't think so,' said Miles. 'Harris said he would not know where to start and that he had a headache coming on. I got the impression that Tony was being held, though?'

'Yes, he is. They think he may be involved in the murders somehow. Harris did not give much away when he rang me.'

'Surely, it's not true, though?'

'How would I know?' She stepped back and shrugged. 'Me and Tony stopped talking months ago. Years ago. Look, I never told you this, Jim, but he's not been right for a long time. He's been obsessed by the death of a former girlfriend. There's always been three of us in the marriage. Me, him and the ghost of the blessed Elaine Murphy.'

Miles stared in amazement as her words came out in a rush.

'I guess I hoped that Tony would eventually move on from her but he didn't,' she said bitterly. 'I've always been a poor replacement for Elaine. Tony always said that he thought Dennis McGuffin had killed her. When he heard a few days ago that the police had reopened the case but were not going to arrest him, he was devastated.'

'My God! Did you tell Dennis?'

'I should have, I suppose, but you know what he was like. There would have been an awful scene. Besides, even when he was murdered I never thought in a million years that Tony could be behind it.'

'You poor thing,' said the vicar and reached out to her.

'I'm going to divorce him. There's no way we can go on like this, and this has been the last straw. Besides, I want to be with you.' She let him hug her as her tears started to fall. 'I guess we're not very good at being honest with each other, are we, love?'

'We'll learn,' he said and kissed her gently on the lips. 'We'll learn.'

'We will,' she said.

'So, do you think they are going to charge Tony?' asked the vicar, letting go of her. 'It explains why they've released Thomas Oldroyd if they are.'

'Harris didn't say. It wasn't a long conversation. You know Jack Harris, he's not a man of many words.'

'You should hear one of his lectures,' said the vicar ruefully. He looked at the wall clock. 'He said there's some sort of meeting. Has it started?'

'Yes, they're in the church.'

Jim Miles headed for the door.

'Best get it over with,' he said. 'But be prepared for the worst. I fear that neither of us will be in a job by the end of it.'

A couple of minutes after Miles and Gerrard had joined the meeting, the two men arrived at St Cuthbert's. After getting out of the car, Thomas Oldroyd and Charlie Daniels stood outside the church for a few moments, their eyes darting left and right in the silence as they sought out movement in the shadows until finally they were content that their arrival had not been noticed. Slowly, cautiously, they pushed their way through the main doors. Daniels was carrying a petrol can. As the door swung slowly shut behind them, a police patrol car pulled up on the road outside the building and the driver reached for his radio.

Inside St Cuthbert's, the men stood and listened to the murmured voices at the far end of the church.

'I think you owe us an explanation,' said Henry Grace, who was chairing the gathering. He looked first at the vicar, then at Anne Gerrard. 'You both do, I think.'

'Yes,' said Edie Prentice, glaring at them. 'Your behaviour leaves an awful lot to be desired and as far as…'

'I think all of us need to do some soul-searching, do we not?' said Grace. He gave her a stern look. 'None of us come out of this with much credit, I would say, Edie.'

'But…'

'Hush your mouth,' said Henry. 'Let them speak.'

'Thank you,' said Miles. 'We are only too acutely aware that our conduct has fallen way below…'

His voice tailed off as Oldroyd stepped forward.

'Good evening, everyone,' he said with a wicked grin on his face in the flickering half-light. He gestured to the petrol can in Daniels's hand. 'I tried to think of something suitably biblical for you and I came up with the fires of Hell. I do hope you approve. It's Charlie's speciality. He would be so disappointed if you didn't like the idea.'

Daniels gave a crooked grin, unscrewed the lid and started sprinkling the petrol over the pews.

'Thomas,' gasped Anne. 'What do you think you're doing?'

Oldroyd surveyed her without emotion then looked at the vicar with undisguised revulsion. He returned his attention to Anne.

'And to think I loved you,' he said with a shake of the head. 'Well, you've made your choice, and now you're going to have to die with the rest of them.'

'Now hang on!' exclaimed Grace, getting to his feet. 'You've already killed Dennis, why kill us?'

Oldroyd walked up to him, boots clicking on the stone floor, the sound of his heels reverberating round the church.

'Because, like you said, you are all culpable.' Oldroyd walked up to Grace until their faces were inches apart. 'You are all guilty of allowing your prejudices to stand in the way of the Lord's work and you must all pay the price. Vengeance is mine, saith the Lord, and vengeance he shall have.'

He glanced at Daniels, who had emptied the can and was fumbling in his jacket pocket for a box of matches. One of the women let out a gasp and Edie Prentice sprang to her feet.

'Now you listen, young man!' she began.

'No, you listen, you silly old fool!' snarled Oldroyd. The sudden explosion of fury shocked them all and, for a few moments, no one spoke. 'You all list…!'

'Thomas Oldroyd!' rang out a voice.

Oldroyd whirled round to see Jack Harris standing at the front door, Gillian Roberts to his right, Matty Gallagher to his left, grim-faced both. Oldroyd looked across to the corridor leading to the office but saw that it was blocked by the burly figure of Grant Wayman, with his arms crossed, and next to him three uniformed officers.

'There's nowhere to run, Thomas,' said Harris.

'You're too late, Chief Inspector,' said Oldroyd. He turned to Daniels only to see that James Larch and Alistair Marshall had walked up quietly behind his startled accomplice and taken the matches and petrol can off him. Daniels did not struggle as Marshall applied the handcuffs.

'I think not,' said Harris.

Oldroyd gave a furious cry and ran up the aisle, surprising the inspector. When he was within a few metres of Harris, Oldroyd produced a knife from his jacket

185

pocket and lashed out at the detective. Recovering his senses, Harris's old army training kicked in, and he swayed inside the blow and slammed a fist into Oldroyd's solar plexus to send him crashing to the floor. The injured man emitted a grunt of pain and struggled to his feet, desperately fighting for breath, then sunk back to his knees and knelt there, his head down as if in prayer.

It was over.

Chapter twenty-four

'I feel that we owe you an apology,' said Gillian Roberts.

She was speaking to David and Judith Fulton as they watched Neil Harker and Jacqueline clamber into the back of the minibus in the police station yard shortly after 11pm.

'Our community has not exactly been welcoming to you,' continued the inspector. She glanced over to the main station building. '*We* have not exactly been welcoming.'

'I wouldn't worry,' said David. 'It comes with the territory. Besides, the killer came from within our number so maybe your suspicions were justified. At least, in part.'

'But you saw through him in the end.'

Fulton looked at his wife.

'Not I,' he said. 'It was Judith. If I had had my way, Thomas Oldroyd would be getting into the bus with us.'

'But surely you would have given him up once you knew what he had done?' said Roberts.

David did not reply.

'My husband's belief in the power of forgiveness is much stronger than mine,' explained Judith. 'I would have done the right thing, of that you can be assured, Inspector.'

'Good.' Roberts watched David fish the ignition keys out of his pocket. 'Where will you go?'

'Wherever the Lord takes us,' he said. 'We will let him guide our journey, as we always do.'

'Maybe the diesel we've given you will allow him to get you further than Preston this time,' said Roberts with a slight smile.

David Fulton smiled in return. It was the first time Roberts could remember seeing him do so. It was good to see.

'Perhaps he was sending us a message,' he continued as he walked round to the driver's side of the vehicle. 'Perhaps he was saying that Preston is our next destination.'

'Pay your credit card bill, that's the only message you're being sent, young man,' said Roberts. 'Anyway, look after yourselves. And look after Neil and Jacqueline. Keep them safe.'

'We will,' said Judith. She climbed into the passenger seat, closed the door and wound down the window. 'It's not an easy life but we'll be OK.'

'I'm sure you will,' said Roberts.

A throaty grumble emanated from the engine as David turned the ignition key and an acrid stench of exhaust fumes filled the yard.

'Keep the faith!' shouted David as the vehicle pulled away.

Matty Gallagher wrinkled his nose at the stench and waved away some of the fumes as he walked up to stand next to the detective inspector. Together, they watched in silence as the minibus lurched onto the street and out of sight. The detectives grinned as the loud report of a backfire echoed across the still night air.

'They'll need all the faith they can get,' said Gallagher. 'I reckon they'll not get further than Carlisle.'

'Perhaps *that's* the Promised Land then.'

'Perhaps it is.' The sergeant looked at her intently. 'Would I be right in suggesting that a small part of you wishes that you were going with them?'

'Nope.' She shook her head emphatically. 'I've done a lot of thinking over the last twenty-four hours, Matty, and that kind of life is not for me. I think it was everyone's prejudice that made me think it was.'

'But you're going to start attending church again, yeah?' said Gallagher. He looked genuinely concerned. 'St Cuthbert's should be a much better place now that Henry Grace is in charge. I'm sure they'd welcome you with open arms. Even Edie, given enough time.'

'What and sit through Jim Miles' sermons?' said Roberts. 'No, I've had enough of that man to last me a lifetime, thank you very much.'

'Yeah, me, too. Henry did hint that they may ask for him to be transferred to another parish. He may be more enlightened than Dennis McGuffin but he still frowns on vicars shagging their secretaries.'

'I'll bet he does,' said Roberts.

'Talking of Henry, I've also been doing a lot of thinking.' The sergeant frowned. 'I made far too many assumptions as well. I mean, I was as wrong as can be over the killer being one of the allotment holders. Suffice to say, I am off Harry Osborne's waiting list.'

'That's a pity but don't beat yourself up about it. It happens to the best of us.' The inspector gave him a rueful smile. 'I can teach you to wallow, if you want.'

'No, thanks. Besides, Harris has already offered.'

'I'll bet he has.' The detective inspector looked round the yard. 'Hey, talking of Hawk, where is he? Has he started on the paperwork?'

'Not quite,' said Gallagher over his shoulder as he started to walk back towards the building. 'In fact, I think you'll find he's doing a spot of worshipping of his own.'

'What does that mean?'

The sergeant opened the rear door to the police station and looked back at her.

'You don't want to know,' he grinned. 'You really don't.'

Roberts watched him disappear into the building.

'No,' she said, 'you're probably right.'

* * *

It was shortly after eleven fifteen when there was a knock on Stella Gaunt's hotel room door. She got out of bed and padded across to open it, revealing Jack Harris standing in the corridor.

'Chief Inspector,' she said.

'Jack will do.' He held up a bottle of whisky. 'I promised you a cup of tea – courtesy of your old pal Grant Wayman.'

'So you did,' said Stella. She opened the door wider to let him in. 'So you did.'

THE END

List of Characters

Superintendent Philip Curtis – divisional commander
Detective Chief Inspector Jack Harris
Detective Inspector Gillian Roberts
Detective Sergeant Matt Gallagher
Detective Constable Alison Butterfield
Detective Constable James Larch
Detective Constable Alistair Marshall

Other police officers

Detective Chief Inspector Grant Wayman - Derbyshire
Police
Detective Constable Stella Gaunt – Leicestershire Police
PC Graham Leckie – uniformed constable with Greater
Manchester Police

Other characters

David Fulton – a Christian
Judith Fulton – his wife
Anne Gerrard – St Cuthbert's church secretary

Tony Gerrard – her husband, editor of the Roxham Herald
Henry Grace – churchgoer
John Halstead – an investigator
Neil Harker – a Christian
Jacqueline – Neil Harker's girlfriend
Dennis McGuffin – Parochial Church Council chairman
The Revd Jim Miles – vicar of St Cuthbert's
Danny Morton – allotment plot holder
Thomas Oldroyd – a Christian
Harry Osborne – allotment committee chairman
Edie Prentice – churchgoer
Zak Raynor – a letting agent

If you enjoyed this book, please let others know by leaving a quick review on Amazon. Also, if you spot anything untoward in the paperback, get in touch. We strive for the best quality and appreciate reader feedback.

editor@thebookfolks.com

www.thebookfolks.com

ALSO BY JOHN DEAN

In this series:

Dead Hill (Book 1)
The Vixen's Scream (Book 2)
To Die Alone (Book 3)
To Honour the Dead (Book 4)
Error of Judgement (Book 6)
The Killing Line (Book 7)
Kill Shot (Book 8)

In the DCI John Blizzard series:

The Long Dead
Strange Little Girl
The Railway Man
The Secrets Man
A Breach of Trust
Death List
A Flicker in the Night
The Latch Man

Made in the USA
Middletown, DE
29 March 2022

63370037R00120